"*All this throws suspicion upon the story. Yet, the element in it that makes the story absurd for reasons based on the facts of existence is more convincing than all the other arguments.*" Ibn Khaldun

"*Make 'em laugh. Make 'em cry. Make 'em wait.*" Charles Dickens (also attributed to Wilkie Collins and Charles Reade)

"*Those who tell the stories rule society.*" Plato

"*The fools think I am writing algebra but what I am really writing is geometry.*" Ernest Hemingway

"*The real voyage of discovery consists not in seeking new landscapes but in having new eyes.*" Marcel Proust

"*The Moving Finger writes; and, having writ,*
Moves on: nor all thy Piety nor Wit
Shall lure it back to cancel half a Line,
Nor all thy Tears wash out a Word of it." Omar Khayyam (translated by Edward Fitzgerald)

The Dabawis and the Shargawis

Faysal Mikdadi

- Lulu.com -

First published in 2013

Printed and distributed through www.lulu.com

Cover design by Faysal Mikdadi

Author's photograph and front cover design by Faysal Mikdadi

ISBN: 978-1-291-26942-0

The Dabawis and the Shargawis   **Faysal Mikdadi**

Faysal Mikdadi (Born in Palestine in 1948) was carried to Lebanon where he was brought up and was given his rather unsuccessful education. He moved to Britain in 1967 and has lived there since. He is an English Literature specialist with a keen interest in the Nineteenth Century Victorian novel and in Shakespeare. His published works include novels, poems, short stories, bibliographies, educational essays and regular contribution on current affairs.

He started writing at a very early age during a turbulent and unhappy childhood. His urge to write comes from a deeply felt need to try to make sense of a disordered and crazy world and to laugh at his own rather stodgy attitudes to a much sought after quiet life. It also comes from his need to laugh at others' predictable higgledy piggledy existence and to celebrate his deep love of nature – the only place in which he sees any order and a semblance of logic.

This collection of short stories and his first musical were composed during Mikdadi's spare time whilst working in Dubai and Ras al Khaimah. His love of both Emirates and his gentle satire shine through these all too human representations.

By the Same Author

Novels:

Chateaux en Palestine, Paris, France, 1982.

Tamra, London, United Kingdom, 1988.

Return, Raleigh NC, USA, 2008.

Snowflake, Raleigh NC, USA, 2013.

Short Stories:

Christmas Stories, Raleigh NC, USA, 2012.

Poetry:

A Return: The Siege of Beirut, London, United Kingdom, 1983.

Bibliographies:

Gamal Abdel Nasser, Westport, USA, 1991.

Margaret Thatcher, Westport, USA, 1993.

Contents

Note from the Author

Between September 2007 and February 2012, I had the good fortune of periodically working in Dubai and Ras al Khaimah in the United Arab Emirates.

I cherish every single moment of my time in both Emirates. For a writer who enjoys constantly observing life around him, both countries gave me a rich tableau of characters each and everyone of whom was a world on their own.

Dubai is indescribably colourful with a truly culturally diverse population. Much of its hustle and bustle brought back memories of my childhood in the Beirut of the fifties and the sixties. Dubai's people are wonderful to be with and to get to know: rich, clever and infuriatingly contrary.

Ras al Khaimah is my little paradise on earth. Its people have a remarkable sensitivity tinged with a great ability to be mischievous and so laugh at themselves – and at everybody else who takes life too seriously – like yours truly.

I made a lot of friends for life in the United Arab Emirates. I hope that nothing in these scribblings offends any of them. These pages are a true reflection of my simple observations, experiences and true renditions of stories heard. Story telling is in our Arab blood.

I hope that Emiratis and other readers enjoy these works of fiction. Enjoyment was my aim in writing them.

Finally, I would like to give a brief explanation of the title of this book to those who have not yet had the good fortune to visit the United Arab Emirates. Dabawis is the old Arabic name for the inhabitants of Dubai, one of the seven Emirates making up the United Arab Emirates. Shargawis is Arabic meaning "those from the east" which was what the inhabitants of Ras al Khaimah were called in the old days. That term has now lapsed and it has been largely replaced by terms such as Emirati, national, local...etc... none of which is as evocative as Shargawis. The letter 'g' is a hard sound as in the letter 'g' in the English word 'guard' or 'go'. For the purists amongst readers, the Orientalist letter used would have been 'q' as being the nearest to the Arabic guttural letter 'qaf'. However, in Lower Egypt, Palestine, Syria and parts of the Arabian Gulf States the Arabic 'q' is often pronounced as a hard 'g'.

Dubai My Dubai: A Counterfeiting

Latin 'fictio': a shaping, a counterfeiting

"History teaches us that the rise and fall of civilisations and the prosperity of peoples and nations are connected to a process of renewal, development and change that includes economic, political, educational, administrative and intellectual reforms.

I understand the frustration at the political and economic failures in our region. I understand our region is under a great deal of pressure, but this pressure should serve as the motivational force to put in extra efforts, to try hard, to strive, to create and to make us more determined to develop and manage our priorities successfully... We should rid ourselves of any frustration or despair and arm ourselves with optimism and hope ..."

H M Mohammad bin Rashid Al Maktoum

Dubai never truly leaves you. It is difficult to say why. A 'new' country with bran new buildings, bran new roads, bran new tallest, longest, widest, deepest and most of everything. A bran new country. Its people ancient with thousands of years of tradition mingling with shallow modern consumerism with all its ugly faces. Dubai never truly leaves you. Even after you have left it for good. And you never know why.

Perhaps it is because of its endless contradictions. Its fathomless natural beauty and deep seated hypocrisy. Perhaps it is because of its wonderful poetry that never ceases to reverberate in the listener's mind even after the poet has taken his bow and gone home. Perhaps its oral tradition of beautiful stories reverberates for so long after departure like a good Beethoven symphony that the listener can never read, replicate or remember fully but that still echoes for years to come.

Perhaps it is the heart-rending image of poorly paid, thin, tired, sweating and bewildered indentured labourers from Bangladesh. Their eyes are so tired, so full of exhaustion that they have little room left for reproach.

It is impossible to explain how a country so bran new, so shiny, so ostentatious and so culturally diverse that it does not project a true national identity, how such a country never truly leaves you.

This brief narrative seeks to understand why.

Before the narrative starts let us shed all the baggage that Dubai loads you with. The infuriating bureaucratic dependence. The inept personal service rarely with a smile and, when with a smile, so put on that it makes you cringe. The social indifference to individual aspirations. The awful rudeness of old age masquerading as the religious duty of the young. The exaggerated reaction to the simplest occurrences. The over reliance on faith to the point of relegating all personal responsibility onto an overworked and obliging God. The tendency never to deliver anything on time. The lack of freedom of expression. The complete and utter disregard for others' feelings. The constant changes of mind by the higher authorities so that the citizen never quite knows what is required of him or her. No need to mention the 'her' really, since women are largely invisible in this man's society where the biggest culprits are not the men but the women themselves for colluding with men's stupidity in the first place. The polite response to the Leader's aspirations without really making the efforts necessary to fulfil his ideal vision. The overt and ugly racism of indigenous Dabawis that permeates their treatment of migrant workers – especially those from India, Pakistan or Bangladesh. And finally, the terrifying way that men and women drive as if it were an offence against nature to allow even a few centimetres of space in between cars grid locked in a traffic jam worsened by bad temper, noise and aggression.

I heard the story from an Arab friend one night when we both sat in an oasis. We were in Al Ain which, strictly speaking, is in neighbouring Abu Dhabi. We had had a wonderful day exploring the glorious local trees and had returned to our hotel exhausted. We had had a sumptuous dinner of Lebanese food and had drunk a little more Arak than we should. We had to smuggle the Arak in for fear of offending our Muslim hosts.

The Dabawis and the Shargawis   Faysal Mikdadi

I must confess to feeling happily tipsy but still relatively in control. My friend appeared a little more sombre and said that he had a little story that he wanted me to read. I felt that I had to read it out of courtesy.

The Arabs do love their story telling... And here is the story that I read to please my Arab friend. Well, I tried to read it but my Dabawi friend kept interrupting me to read a bit aloud or to expand on the narrative a little further. Unnecessarily, I must add, for the narrative spoke for itself. See what you think, *dear reader*.

****

"I would be mortified if you never returned to Dubai." She spoke softly, her New York accent mellifluously undulating amongst the bran new furniture in a large hall – so softly that he could hardly hear her.

"But I have to. I have a new contract and it is well paid. And I need the money. I need lots of money. Mammon calls. We can still get together during the summer holidays."

"I would be mortified if you decided to leave. Do you really need money? I can let you have some. Do you need money?"

"I don't like Dubai. I like my quiet English country life. My slow motion existence in rural Dorset. I like my trees and my garden. I don't like Dubai's noise and endless pursuit of wealth. It sickens me. I want to go home."

"Pursuit of wealth? And you talk of Mammon calling?"

"Yes, but that's a gentle British Mammon and not a fraud like Dubai's society. A sham. A meaningless and shallow world."

She looked at him sitting before her with his bottom lip trembling like a homesick five year old yearning for his mum.

She touched his hand gently and squeezed it spasmodically.

"I say, old girl, anybody observing us would think that you are in love with me. Hey, old thing, we're not falling in love with each other, are we? I do love my wife you know."

"I know. You are an adorable bore who is viciously loyal to her with her big blue eyes and her pretty blonde hair, aren't you?"

He did not answer her. He stared into space as his eyes filled and his bottom lip trembled. He felt so childishly homesick.

They sat in the large hall with their whispers echoing quietly. She pointed to a line of office workers walking rigidly on the other side of the glass.

"Look at all those people utterly oblivious of God's presence. It breaks my heart to see them walking in their sleep." Her eyes were wide with pity.

"What are you talking about? These people are decent practising Muslims. They know God very well, thank you very much." His own eyes were wide with shock at her apparent intolerance.

"Not the true God. They know Allah, whatever that is. Theirs is not a real faith. It has nothing to do with our Lord Jesus Christ."

"Oh, I so love your American Evangelism. It shines forth like a beacon of hope for all of us sinners…"

"Don't mock."

"I mock thee not. I too feel sorry for those who appear to be lost. That's the majority of us. But I wouldn't dream of telling them that Jesus is the only true Lord. When we all come before Him, I shall plead for those people's souls if they were wrong in their faith during their short lives on this adorable little globe. I shall ask Him to look at their good deeds as a token of their goodness."

"Good deeds mean nothing. You are either with God or you are in another place. That's it. Nothing else matters."

"What? Good deeds do not matter?"

"Of course they don't. They are very nice in themselves but they have nothing to do with being in the same place as God."

" *'For as the body without the spirit is dead, so faith without works is dead also.'* "

"That's often misquoted."

" *'Inasmuch as ye have done it unto one of the least of these my brethren, ye have done it unto me .'* "

"That, too, is often misunderstood..."

"Yes, of course, Jesus was an American Evangelist milking your purse for all its worth, peddling unreadable crap."

"Jesus was a good Jew."

"A Palestinian Jew to boot."

"There were never any Palestinians. That is a modern construct thrown in by Muslims to deny Jews their homeland."

"Oh, I see. So our colleague Mariam was not born in Nazareth. Her father did not farm near Netanyah. Her mother must have been a figment of her imagination."

"Don't be ridiculous. Our Lord promised Palestine to the Jews. The Arabs invaded whole swathes of the Middle East by force and called it theirs. So the poor Jews had to wander for two thousand years."

"Oh I see. So God has set Himself up as an estate agent. And He presumably promised America to the white European settlers after those Native American savages invaded it. And he promised England to the French who then took it square and fair in 1066... You do talk rot, my dear."

Her eyes blazed at him as her face distorted with anger. She pointed at him and looked as if she was about to explode. Suddenly, she looked away with wide eyes straining for control. After a while she turned to him and asked.

"What are you doing this weekend?"

"Nothing. Writing silly poems."

"Your poems are never silly... Do you want to spend the weekend with me?"

He feigned a look of shock and horror.

"Separate rooms," she said impatiently. "Do you want to spend the weekend with me?"

"Where?"

"Al Ain."

"Where is that?"

"What difference does it make. It is not far from here. I want you to come there for the weekend and then decide whether you will take the new contract in England or not."

"Why?" he asked, his bottom lip still trembling slightly.

"Because I want to make up for the hurts of the five year old, the hurts of the fifteen year old, the hurts of the twenty five year old, the hurts of the thirty five year old, the hurts of the forty five year old, the hurts of the fifty five year old. Each and every hurt that the five year old boy had to receive all through his long life. God bless him."

"What's God got to do with it? This five year old's destiny is in his hands and his hands alone. God gave him the tools and the manual and told him to go and get on with it."

"Don't blaspheme. Do you want to spend the weekend with me in Al Ain?"

"Okay. I would love to spend the weekend with you in Al Ain. Do you mean '*country matters*', my lady?" he smirked at her mischievously.

"You really love smashing little icons, don't you?"

"Who? Me? Never!"

"Meet you in the lobby of your hotel at five on Thursday," she ordered.

****

The taxi driver alternated between gloomy silence and voluble outbursts. With his left hand on the wheel, his right hand busily choreographed his every utterance and underlined his every meaning.

"And so, here we are. Both refugees. You from Britain and I from Syria. And what do we get here in Dubai? Work, more work and more work. And very little pay. I barely clear five hundred a month. Up with the dawn. I pray, break my fast and I am off to work. The mobile never stops ringing. He is checking on me to see that I am where I am supposed to be. He is a Palestinian and doesn't trust anyone. No wonder after what those bastards did to his homeland. And who cares? Certainly not that vicious heathen Obama. He comes in full of promises and does nothing. He wouldn't dare, the rotten coward. Last time someone tried to understand us Arabs, the Israelis killed him. Kennedy was killed by the Jewish lobby you know. What chance have we got against those people? The Jews hate us. And the Christians do what the Jews tell 'em to do all the time. What can we do about it? Nothing. If we tried, the authorities arrest us and torture us like they did my brother-in-law in Aleppo. He disappeared for weeks. They hanged him upside down until he promised never to say anything against the regime. I swear to you. That was what they did. I know. I saw him when he came back. With cigarette burns all over his – excuse me for saying it – all over his balls. How could they? And then when Frenchmen kill Germans on French soil, they are called heroes. When Iraqis kill British soldiers on Iraqi soil, they are charged with murder and tried. And when Lebanese kill an Israeli soldier on Lebanese soil they are called terrorists. The world has gone upside down my brother."

A long silence followed punctuated with a sharp exhalation of breath accompanied by a raised right arm that stopped in mid air with palms upwards before turning itself over and, like a gifted acrobat, sliding through the air and landing with a loud and expressive thud against the taxi driver's thigh.

"We Muslims are not bad people. We work hard. We look after our families. We do things our way. We don't do any harm. Just because the West doesn't like our faith, it hates us. Why can't they see the injustice that they have done to the Palestinians in Palestine? Why do they support Israel without even asking any questions whatever she does? You might understand why. You live in Britain. Why do they hate us so much? Now Iran can't have a nuclear weapon but it is all right for Israel to have hundreds. Saddam disobeyed the UN so they lynched him. Israel has never even once obeyed one of the hundreds of UN resolutions reprimanding it. But that's okay. The Jews can do whatever they want. Why do they hate us so much?"

The passenger grunted a few times and remained silent. The driver's right arm went up in the air, twirled around and landed on his thigh before he continued his tirade.

"I know. I know. No one has the answer. But then all those Western leaders who do everything that they can to support Israel against us and then, when they leave office and have no power anymore, they start speaking for the right of the Palestinians. Look at Carter. Do you remember him? He was president for four years and did nothing for us. Now he is our friend. Look at Clinton. When he wasn't busy doing rude things with cigars, he did everything to blame us for the failed peace talks. Now he is a good friend who believes there should be a Palestinian state. And that white man's slave Kofi Anan. Listen to him telling us that the Palestinian issue must be resolved if the world is to live in peace. Where was he when Israel was murdering Palestinians and Lebanese by their thousands? They are all cowards. Running scared of the Jewish lobby. Cowards. But never mind my brother. Never mind. Allah will deliver us, insh'Allah..."

The right hand became very active for a few long minutes, rising, twirling and falling down with a thud.

"Never mind my brother. Allah is watching. He will not tolerate this injustice. He will correct it. He is a just God. He is a loving God but He is also a just God who will punish the infidel for treating his children so badly. He will punish them. They say that Jesus will come again to Jerusalem and punish the Jews. Even the Christians think that what they have done in Palestine is wrong but they still help the Jews. A Nazarene from Lebanon told me that the Christians believed that the Jews needed to come back to Palestine so that they could all be in one place so that God could then send Jesus and punish them for forgetting his orders and doing things in the wrong way. You see, even their own people believe that they are criminals. And Israel is so clever, it is using all of this to keep the Christian West on its side. They think that we are ignorant. We know. We know. But we are too busy working every hour that God sent in order just to survive. I barely clear five hundred Dirhams a month. And most of it goes to my wife in our Syrian village. We have a small plot of land where she grows vegetables. I asked her to join me here in Dubai with the children. She did not want to. Who can blame her? Heat and dust. Nothing but heat and dust. And grinding poverty. I have been here twenty three years. I go home for a month every year. We have ten children. After the tenth visit she started making a fuss about me using those horrible rubbery things. I ask you? What's the point of taking your wife without producing? What does the good Lord say?"

What the good Lord said was left a secret as the driver exhaled noisily and allowed his right arm to dance a lengthy solo as the car slowly started to glide to a halt outside the hotel. The passenger rolled five one hundred Dirham notes and clumsily shoved them into the driver's shirt pocket. He ran up the hotel steps as the driver's words of gratitude scurried after him.

****

"What a great ride. I had the pleasure of hearing a lengthy lecture from a Syrian street professor."

"What did he have to say for himself?"

"Oh I love that New York accent that is even more heavily accented when you are about to be judgmental."

"I am not judgmental. I just asked you what he had to say for himself."

The Dabawis and the Shargawis   Faysal Mikdadi

He tried to summarise what the taxi driver had said, occasionally unsuccessfully imitating his Syrian accent and the twirl of the right arm. She did not laugh.

"It's disgusting. It really is. Those Muslims with their fake faith. They really believe this crap. It breaks my heart to see them conned like that. I pray fervently every night for them to see the truth and be with the Lord. You are either with the Lord or you are not. It is very simple." She looked into space with wide eyes, as she drove apparently distractedly down the straight new highway.

"So no judgement there then. Good. I am pleased to see that. Which Lord are we talking about then?" He asked.

"The only One. The Lord Jesus Christ. He is the only one."

"What gave you a monopoly on truth? May be the Muslims have got it right."

"No they haven't. Don't be stupid. Have you read the lies that their so-called Holy Qur'an has to say. The position is very simple. First there were the Jews. And then our Lord Jesus came to validate the laws and not to amend them. And that's where we are now."

"You mean that superbly crafty *Sermon on the Mount* when He tells us that He is not come to destroy the laws but to fulfil them and then He proceeds to change every single one of them."

"He does not change them. He develops them."

"And Mohammad develops them a step further in the final message."

"No he doesn't. He came too late to do anything. He was fake. You know, like a five dollar bill. There is the real article and the fake one. They look alike. But the fake one is a fake. And that is Islam."

"Wow, your American Evangelism is breathtaking. I do hope that you do not share your views with colleagues in Dubai."

"I am a visitor here. I am not going to offend anyone. I just feel sorry for them for not having the true faith. My heart goes out to them. Poor things."

"If it upsets you that much why don't you bugger off back to the good old US of A and settle happily in its Christian lands away from the heathen Muslims? Honestly, old girl, you are talking right wing bollocks. I presume you learnt it all on the knee of a good Mossad agent when he was visiting lovely Dubai to plan the murder of Palestinian visitors!"

"Shut up and enjoy the drive to Al Ain."

****

Al Ain. Strangely, it reminded him of Tunbridge Wells. There was no resemblance whatsoever. It just did.

The two sat in an oasis of trees that appeared to go as far as the eye could see.

"This is magnificent. It really is so beautiful. Thank you for bringing me here old girl. It is out of this world."

"I thought that you'd like it. So green, isn't it?"

"Yes. There is nothing like nature. It is so beautiful. When I look at this, for the first time, I understand Wordsworth's Pantheism."

"What's that? Pantheism?"

"The idea that God is in nature."

"But God is in everything. There is no such thing as Mother Nature. That's a Darwinian cop out. God is the creator of everything and the controller of everything."

"Please, my dearest and most beloved friend, cut the God stuff. Please. Don't spoil this special moment of communing with nature."

"You're not communing with nature. You're communing with God."

"If you say so. I don't care what you call it. Just let me enjoy it."

"I don't call 'it' anything. I see it for what it is: God's wonderful creation."

"So all comes from God?"

"Of course."

"If that is the case, what about the Italian earthquake? What was that? A little present for Signor Berlusconi?"

"Don't blaspheme. The earthquake was a punishment from God. A punishment against the Catholic Church that had lost its way."

"A bit harsh. A little vindictive."

"He is a just God."

"Surely, He is a forgiving God..."

"Of course! He is a loving God but He is also a just God who will withdraw his blessing from those who abandon Him like the Italian Catholics".

"Tell that to the families of all those who died."

"We shouldn't question what God does or wills. We should only be thankful."

"For a nice little earth quake?"

"We should be thankful. I have a friend in Arizona whose husband and son were killed in a car crash. I was there when they told her the news. She went straight on her knees and gave The Lord thanks for all the blessings that He had given her. She was blessed."

"I would rather do without that blessing. Come on. If it happened to me I would rant and rave for years."

"He doesn't mind you ranting and raving as long as you do not blaspheme."

"You live in a mad world dearest heart."

"And you live in a faithless one away from God. You know, every night, I kneel and pray that our Lord Jesus enter your heart. He will."

"Meanwhile, I am assuming that He is preparing a little earthquake somewhere else where they have pissed Him off?"

"Somewhere where He wishes to withdraw His Blessing."

"Well, old girl, put in a good word for your little friend..."

"I do. Every night."

"You think of me at night?"

"Yes. You are in my prayers. Don't you think of me?"

"Yes. As I lie on my back fantasising about what I would like to do to you..."

"You're disgusting. But I love you to bits still."

"Good thing, in case He's listening."

****

The two sat in the midst of trees savouring the cool breeze wafting gently through the huge palm leaves. The recent rains had left that delicious smell that can only come from the desert sand. It filled them with an inner warmth too glorious to disturb with any talk.

It brought back memories of childhood: warm, innocent and trouble free. As if both had been babes in the desert.

"I have understood what you're saying love. But I can't subscribe to it for now. This is so beautiful that I don't want to label it as God's creation or God's bounty. It feels so artificial. Can't I just enjoy it as I do my poetry? Just let it seep through me and fill me with a love of something?"

"Of course you can. It is probably filling you with the love of our Lord. But you don't know it yet."

"Why did you say that bit about Darwin being a con or something like that?"

"Because that was exactly what he was. His theory was utterly wrong. The story of the creation is quite clearly told in *Genesis*. Darwin is talking nonsense. Apart from anything else, if we are descended from some slimy creepy crawly or from an ape, that means that our Lord did not need to come down to save us from our sins and to do away with death. It would mean that we are accidental. That we simply came from a developmental process that had nothing to do with our Lord. This is patent nonsense."

"Darwin's theory is so elegant. So perfect. *The Old Testament* story is a myth. Some kind of silly story passed on from father to son. You don't really believe it, do you?"

"The story of the creation is literal. It happened exactly as told. *The Holy Scriptures* are literal. Go to them for the truth."

"For goodness' sake love. You are not serious? All these idiotic miracles, incestuous relationships, murders, thefts, battles, killings, genocide... Come on. And the idiotic promise to Abraham which those Israeli expansionist fascists want us to believe gave them Palestine? The British stole and gave them Palestine, the Russians armed them and then the Americans became their stooges who would do anything for a small group of invaders stealing somebody else's land just as they themselves had done in North America. And you want us to believe that God promised them that?"

"Of course He did."

"Yes, of course He did. And then, for two thousand years, he stuck Palestinians on the land so that European and American Jews could come in and kill them and dispossess them just for the hell of it. That's the just God who is willing to sit and watch over eight million Palestinians living in the Diaspora or under vicious Israeli occupation. And what about his promise to Abraham about his other son?"

"What promise?"

"*And as for Ishmael, I have heard thee: Behold, I have blessed him, and will make him fruitful, and will multiply him exceedingly; twelve princes shall he beget, and I will make him a great nation.'* And in another place, '*And also of the son of the bondwoman will I make a nation, because he is thy seed.'* And again, '*Arise, lift up the lad, and hold him in thine hand; for I will make him a great nation.'* Come on! What great nation? The Arabs? Wow! I am glad he didn't make me that promise. Anyhow, Ishmael lived in the wilderness and became an archer. Then he married an Egyptian. Great nation indeed. Look at the poor buggers. Not even the dignity of independence. Israel rules the Egyptian weaklings."

"You are talking politics. This has nothing to do with *The Holy Scriptures.*"

"Oh! I see. So when it is to do with Israel and the so-called 'Promise', then it is scriptural truth. When it is to do with the Palestinians or Arabs, it is politics. Now I understand. If you will excuse me, I really do not wish to continue this moronic discussion made up of pure double standards like all things Christian or Western..."

A long silence followed.

She softly recited with a gentle look on her face.

"*Stop all the clocks, cut off the telephone,*

Prevent the dog from barking with a juicy bone,

Silence the pianos and with muffled drum

Bring out the coffin, let the mourners come."

"It's so beautiful. Very touching," he said.

"Of course it is. It is about real love. A man mourning the death of his loved wife."

"No it isn't. It is a man mourning the death of his beloved lover – another man."

"It isn't. Don't spoil it."

"Why should that spoil it? It is still about love. '*He was my North, my South, my East and my West. My working week and my Sunday rest. My noon, my midnight, my talk, my song. I thought that love would last forever, I was wrong.*' They loved each other. That's all."

"It is an abomination unto the Lord. Anyhow, love does last forever. For eternity. It is not just for now. It is for eternity with God. Make that choice. And you will be all right. Homosexuality is an abomination unto the Lord."

"Oh dear. Here we go again. Love is love is love is love. I don't remember Jesus saying anything about gay people."

"You will see, when *The End of Days* comes and when it is *The Trembling of the Cup*..."

"For goodness' sake. Listen to yourself. Stephen Dedalus's priests have nothing on you. Anyhow, *The End of Days* is a Hebraic prophecy that suits Israel's expansionist policy magnificently. And *The Trembling of the Cup* is from Isaiah's letter to those in Babylonian captivity urging them not to give in to sensuality and materialism. You know, he might as well write to the Dabawis, the Americans and the British. Or the cup overfloweth and we will have a credit crunch... You are sick old bean. So bloody intolerant. A right wing Evangelist."

"I am not. I have taken these things to the Lord and He has guided me."

"Has He? Well that's big of Him. So big. Bully for Him. And I presume that He is a fully fledged citizen of the great US of A."

"Go to *The Holy Scriptures*. You will find the answer there."

"You mean like those morons *The Bereans*. Those pernicious hate peddlers who are about as Christian as my left foot! They don't even know the meaning of Christian love with their venomous hatred of everyone who does not agree with them. People led by a man whose only motive is profit. For goodness' sake, every time he talks, he recommends one of his ghastly organisation's products. He must be making millions from gullible fools like you."

"Please don't talk like that. They are right. Go to *The Holy Scriptures*. *The Holy Scriptures* have the answer. Always."

"No old girl. I would rather go for a long walk and commune with nature."

"There is no nature."

"No nature?"

"No nature."

"And what are these magnificent trees?"

"God's creations."

"Nature is God's creation."

"I hate this reference to nature. It is all God. There is no nature."

"Oh, I love that Shakespearean stichomythia. Reminds me of Macbeth and his Mrs. chatting after the deed was done. Short, staccato utterances. Like yours. 'There is no nature.' Hmm! You are terrifying. Like Lady Macbeth."

"And you are Macbeth?"

"Feels like it…"

"Then '*screw your courage to the sticking place*' and find God."

"Oh! I'm impressed. You can quote the Old Bard. But no thank you my dear. I would rather commune with nature…"

"And nature is God."

"Okay. Shit smells as foul by any other name…"

"Don't!"

"Sorry love," he said abruptly.

He got up and walked away from her. She watched him a little while, put her hands together and appeared to pray fervently. After a while, she got up and walked back towards the hotel.

****

He continued to walk until he found himself in a rounded opening in the middle of the trees. The shade was so cool. He felt intensely happy. He stood in the middle looking around him at the way that the sand undulated in little pretty hillocks.

The man appeared from nowhere.

He stood on top of one of the small mounds looking out. His eyes moved slowly until they landed on the man standing in the middle of the circle.

He walked down towards him.

He had what appeared to be an old wrap around and no shoes. He walked without noise and did not seem to be affected by external factors like the hot sun or the small stones that he walked on with ease.

"Hello," came the voice from the middle of the circle.

"Hello," replied the visitor.

"Beautiful place. Really magnificent."

"Yes... It is... Always has been from the first day of Creation."

"I expect it was. Some things are too beautiful to change."

"Like her faith?"

"What do you mean?"

"I overheard your conversation. She is right you know. That's why I am here. She is right. I have been waiting for you for a long time."

"You're not serious? I suppose in a minute you are going to do a little jig, deliver a telegram and run off…" The speaker sounded a little nervous.

"Don't disbelieve what you see. All gods are dead. I am the only One. I am the Light. I have been waiting for you for a long time."

"Why me?"

"You are a good man. And you are right. Good deeds do matter. But they shine all the more done in My Name. They bless infinitely more done with Me in your heart. Come. You can choose. You said yourself. I've given you the manual and the tools. Now come, make your choice. It is for the best."

"Can I ask you something?"

"Yes."

"Why do horrible things happen to us? Why do You allow it?"

"I have given you the tools and the manual. All that you have is good. It is for you to make the choices. And when things go badly, don't look to me for the cause. Look to yourselves. I have given you The Kingdom of Heaven. No wrong can happen there. All that goes wrong does so because you will it."

"I thought that You willed everything."

"No. I will no evil. I told you. Using your words. I gave you the tools, I gave you the manual and I let you get on with it. You choose. It's very simple."

"It feels different. Good somehow."

"Don't be embarrassed by it. Enjoy it."

"But it's so embarrassing. You know. To believe in things you can not prove."

"'*There are more things in heaven and earth, than are dreamt of in your philosophy*'..."

"You're good. My favourite author..."

"I thought that you would understand... Come. Come with me. Come."

He turned and walked back towards the small hill. He started to climb it effortlessly. He looked back once and smiled.

In the middle of the circle, the man went down on his knees and held his head in his hands. A warm sensation permeated his heart. He looked up at the disappearing figure and smiled broadly.

"I will come with You..." he whispered without moving.

****

She sat quietly staring ahead of her. He watched her with real warmth in his heart. He wondered if he could tell her about his experience. Would she believe him? He smiled to think that not only would she believe him, she would probably break forth into some embarrassing celebratory song. They would join hands and kneel together to give thanks to The Lord.

No. He could not do it. It would be far too embarrassing. Rather like those dreams of appearing at the company meeting or seminar and realising that one is stark naked. Of course, the beauty of these dreams is that nobody seems to be bothered about, or shamed by, his nakedness. Except for him. Yet, the seminar would have to continue and he would stand there delivering his piece in his birthday suit before waking up in a cold sweat.

What a bizarre analogy to describe meeting Jesus Christ.

Had he really done so?

What else could it be?

He was a practical, pragmatic and scientific chap for whom all faith was an inherent human weakness. A kind of Marxist '*opiate of the people* '. It was convenient for keeping the masses in their places. And in the Britain of today it was replaced by football and other moronic sporting activities. Or, even worse, by cretinous reality shows or celebrity icons showing human weaknesses at their most pathetic and at their ugliest.

And there he was. Full of warmth and happiness at what he saw.

Faith was an affair of the heart really. Nothing to do with reason or logic. Perhaps that was the answer.

"Are you all right?" she asked.

The Dabawis and the Shargawis   **Faysal Mikdadi**

"Yes, old girl. Perfectly all right."

"You look different."

"In what way?"

"I don't know. You look so relaxed. Almost happy. You are not so tense. Your communing with nature has obviously done you good. Trees always do that to you. That was why I brought you to Al Ain."

"Was it?"

"Yes. I thought that you would be in your element here…"

He smiled at her and suddenly realised how beautiful she was. She had the biggest eyes he had ever seen. What the Arabs call 'al taraf al aghar' meaning 'the tempting corner'. From the corner of a cow's eyes looking up in that inordinately innocent way. 'Al taraf al aghar' was the Arabic origin of Trafalgar.

She was again staring into space with those huge glistening brown eyes. Occasionally, her pretty little nose twitched almost imperceptibly as she blinked seemingly ever so slowly. He suddenly realised that her eyes blinking were a little like the dying Bambi. They were slightly wet and shone in the distance. Her mouth looked severe until she moved her eyes and caught his. She smiled.

Her smile lit up the entire oasis where they sat drinking coffee. It fitted utterly with the perfect lightness in his heart.

He smiled back and gently took her delicate little hand. He could not quite believe that these dainty little fingers belonged to a fully-grown adult. They reminded him of a child as they gently squeezed his index finger.

"You really do look different," she said.

"I feel different," he replied as they walked towards the hotel entrance.

Once inside, he turned and faced her.

"What is it?"

"Nothing," he replied.

"Something has happened. What is it? Please tell me."

He did not reply. He pulled her towards him and held her against him.

"Thank you," he whispered.

She held him fiercely as if he were an illusion she was about to lose.

And suddenly she realised what it was. She realised what had happened. And she knew that there would never be any parting between them.

They walked up the stairs to collect their luggage for the return drive to Dubai. He, gliding with Ecstasy. She, floating with unending happiness.

****

The two stood in the hotel foyer. The concierge was making an awful fuss of a small bag being placed in the back of the hotel's gleaming white Lexus.

"I love you to bits. Stay." She faltered.

"I, too, love you to bits."

"Stay then."

"I won't stay."

"Why? I don't understand."

"I want to be with my wife. I want my old life back."

"Then we will live where you want. I'll sell everything and come and live in your bookish mess. All I ask is that you let me keep my faith. I could not live without you."

"No. It won't work. I'm sorry. Your faith is cruel, intolerant and malicious. It has nothing to do with the gentility of Jesus. It has nothing to do with tolerance of a kind Lord. It has nothing to do with forgiveness and love. It is full of hate masquerading as justice. Full of venom masquerading as God's will. Full of malice masquerading as *Old Holy Testament* values. Yours is not my world. There is no difference between you and all those believing in other faiths and in no faiths whose cruel behaviour you so deplore. "

"I love you to bits."

"I love you too."

"I don't understand."

"Good bye. God bless you."

****

I looked up from the script. My Dabawi friend was fast asleep. I must confess to feeling awfully sleepy myself. Especially after such a silly story. So unlikely.

I must admit, I still find it difficult to believe the story. The Arabs do love to tell a good tale. Well, it was an evening's entertainment. Not that I was particularly entertained by this silly and improbable piece of fiction. But the food was glorious and the Arak absolutely divine.

Why do I say improbable? My Dabawi friend swore that the story was true. '*Whenever you have eliminated the impossible, whatever remains, however improbable, must be the truth*'. Isn't this the principle by which that great private detective, Sherlock Holmes, lived? I do not know.

That is why Dubai never leaves you. Even after you have left it. And I left it a long time ago after becoming very ill. I spent six months in a lonely hospital ward. But that is another story.

No wonder most of the world's religions were born in this part of the world. It is as it should be. Both a blessing and a curse. Depends how you choose to live it.

But then don't trust a silly story to make a decision about Dubai. Go there yourself. Let go of all that you are and all that you know. Let Dubai take you in. And you will never be the same again.

Because Dubai never leaves you. It makes you in its image and you are trapped. For good.

And you will then believe the unbelievable.

Honest.

Blue Eyes Do Not a White Woman Make

"I am Egyptian. My mother was Egyptian. I am now Emirati. My father was Emirati..."

I smiled politely straining hard to summon a convincing modicum of interest where none existed.

"No one believes I'm Arab."

I looked so absorbed and aptly dying for more of this fascinating information.

"'Cause of my blue eyes..."

And she fluttered her large blue eyes at me. I looked appropriately amazed at such phenomenal beauty.

I wanted to reply that I was British but nobody believed that I was British because I had a puckered little brown face and other bits. I refrained from sharing this delightful piece of information and looked up at her and smiled in appreciation at her wonderful social skills.

"Yes doctor. And I am married."

My facial muscles were beginning to ache from assumed postures that were not second nature to me.

"And I have two boys."

Well, that was a real shock to me. A real shock.

"And no one believes that I have two boys because I am so slim." Her hands slid down her sides and over her straight buttocks. And I opened my eyes wide at this seventh wonder of the world.

"Yes doctor... It is amazing. And my sister works in finance over there. You interviewed her. She is very dark." She wrinkled her pretty little nose with distaste at anyone being remotely dark.

I tried very hard to look white. But I only looked like my little face, brown through and through.

"Your English is so beautiful doctor. If I shut my eyes and listened, I would think you blond."

I smiled and wished that she would shut her mouth instead.

"You must visit us doctor. Bring your wife. Do you have a picture of her?"

I went into my I-Phone and showed her a photograph of Susan sent two days ago: sitting in the car, flashing a huge smile and showing very blonde hair luxuriating against her bright red coat.

"Ah! Aaah! Ah!" she moaned. "A real blonde with blue eyes."

She wriggled her body from top to bottom and closed her legs tightly.

Now, that I appreciated for I do the same when my wife smiles at me.

"What is her name?" she asked breathlessly.

"Susan."

"Soooooooozaaaaaaan!" She whispered as she sat back with her eyes shut.

And I thought it a wonderful coincidence that Susan had the same effect on me - in the privacy of our boudoir, of course.

She opened her large blue eyes that were glistening on the edge of tears. She looked imploringly at me with regret glinting in her irises. For not being blonde, I assumed.

The intercom on her desk went. She bent forward and clicked the switch. There was an incomprehensible female grunt that she nodded to. She flipped the intercom off, sat up, adjusted her large head scarf repeatedly and stood up briskly.

"The Director will see you now, doctor. This way please."

And we walked briskly and determinedly as post coital couples do after the deed - in search of normal life that bears not the remotest resemblance to their inner desires.

Happy Occasion

"Forssah saïda," he intoned as he chewed peanuts and fingered his mobile. His eyes never looked up at the visitor who had given such claimed joy. His hands fiddled with the earpiece as he adjusted it to better hear what he was secretly listening to. The visitor, a rather stodgy Briton, stood uncomfortably trying to make eye contact with eyes that were elsewhere. The secretary smiled embarrassedly and invited him to sit down. Meanwhile, the man continued fiddling with his mobile and shutting out the world. He kept intoning inanities to no one in particular as the visitor wondered who on earth he was. The visitor asked for an appointment to see the Head of Section. Before the secretary could even answer, "This evening," ejaculated the fiddler. The visitor mumbled apologies. Prior engagement. Regret. Perhaps next week. "Forssah saïda," sang the man as he waddled out of the room still not looking up. "I'll pick my certificate up later," he shouted over his shoulder. His feet hardly came off the ground as he shuffled his way down the corridor. The visitor smiled at the secretary wondering if she had a voice. He said his thank yous and departed more confused than when he arrived. The internecine arcana of this visit was beyond his inflexible capabilities. He walked out to the foyer and occupied his time following the colour codes to each office. All four colours worked and took him to his desired destination. The fifth colour, yellow, took him nowhere. He bumped into the Director's secretary who waved burning incense around him and by his face. He refrained from asking where the yellow line went as he turned around and speedily walked to his temporary office, opened the window just as he started a severe coughing fit that rasped his throat and congested his chest.

The yellow brick road indeed!

The Dabawis and the Shargawis　　　　　　　**Faysal Mikdadi**

At last, je ne regrete rien, taqreeban[1]

The five school inspectors arrived punctually. In itself, a meaningless happenstance. In Dubai's morning traffic, a veritable miracle.

Monsieur le directeur stood by the resplendent fluttering French flag. He puffed his chest out in wonderful French pride. The lead inspector, Dr. Parker, swept towards him, arms spread wide, steps firm and mouth stentoriously uttering loud greetings.

This was destined to be a visit of stereotypes. Every conceivable delightful French stereotype would step forth, be recognised, labelled, loved and passed by. Oh, the sheer the joy of Francophilia. It drips like Manna from Heaven and washes the past away. In its place, dawns la France. Glorious. Grand. Alive. And so Proustian, it is divine.

Parker walked briskly imagining that he could march to a loud and lusty "Allons enfants de la Patrie le jour de gloire est arrivé..." And as he approached Monsieur Dupont, he fancied that he could smell le café, la Gauloise and he could hear Jean Paul Sartre intoning softly. His mind raced back to 1966 in Paris. He was eighteen years old and a rabid existentialist.

---

[1]　　Arabic for 'nearly' or 'almost'.

Ah, God was dead. Long live Logic. Long live my good deeds. "Aux armes citoyens…" Let us, Français et Française, go forward and change the world. It is all we have to work with. Let not that wonderful opium of the masses eat your brain out and convince you otherwise. God is a soporific to shut you up.

Look what we achieved mes amis. Vietnam is gone and recognised as an inhuman mistake. The Berlin Wall came and went. That evil empire the Soviet Union has become history. And now we are able to be ourselves. Speak freely. Laugh loudly. And we showed the world how unkind it had been to women and told women to bare their breasts and be happy. And we make love every time the urge takes us. Who needs God?

And now Parker was a sixty year old rabid existentialist.

Monsieur Dupont pumped the Parker hand with determined rigour. The two men walked into the school followed by the other four inspectors remaining utterly unacknowledged.

The four walked slightly tentatively for fear of appearing to intrude into Parker's magnificent daydream. They were clearly fascinated by his chameleon like adaptability. They smiled at each other fondly. Good chap Parker. Works hard and means well. His heart drips nothing but kindness and it pumps it out by the quart. He leaves a trail of happiness wherever he goes.

Of the four inspectors, one was a British fusspot who had thoroughly learnt the absolute importance of being earnest. One was Lebanese and had a delightful and forceful volubility. One was a German married to a Russian Princess half his age. And the fourth was a Belgian with piercing blue eyes and the softest shoulders Parker had ever seen.

And the inspection began to unfold as it always did.

Monsieur le président arrived with due decorum. He spoke slowly and deliberately. His words were complex and his sentences straight out of Victor Hugo's prose. His financial explanations sent shivers of terror down his listener's spine. Parker loved listening to him explaining the intricacies of the French education system and its attendant ministry of this and ministry of that.

Monsieur le vice président, occasionally stealing cautious glances at monsieur le président, spoke in a heavy smoker's deep rasping guttural voice. He gave a lengthy history of the school, its board and its tortured finances. Parker, to all invisible viewers, looked as if he was listening to *La Comédie Humaine*.

The Dabawis and the Shargawis   **Faysal Mikdadi**

Then came the parents.

The three parents, a French woman, a Canadian and an Egyptian, spoke fast and with considerable confidence about their children's education. This indeed was the day of stereotypes. The Egyptian was covered from head to toe. Her scarf was so severe that Parker averted his gaze. His eyes fell on the French woman's almost exposed breasts. As she bent towards him to explain her views on education, both breasts fell forward and Parker quickly averted his gaze back to the Egyptian severity. His modesty was short lived as he returned to feast on the beautiful scenery. His eyes devoured every detail down to the sweet rounded nipples. Overwhelming shame moved his eyes to the Canadian's face which nodded gently at him as if to reassure him that his tender weakness was excusable for these, indeed, were magnificent breasts. Impartially speaking of course. *La Joconde.*[2] Vous voilá!

Discussion after discussion after discussion continued to the accompaniment of endless bitter black coffee, crispy fluffy croissants and a pile of Palmiers. Parker's deep seated love for the occasional well rounded firm breast was only overtaken by his passion for reading Proust and munching sweet Palmiers. Never mind the Madeleine Cakes mon vieux. Give Parker a Palmier any day. Being a diabetic, this passion would prove fatal one day. But for now, the

---

2   *The Mona Lisa.*

excess sugar made base camp around his rotund belly and back overlooking a pert tight little bottom.

Parker had fallen in love recently. But, more of that anon as the story tellers say.

He had been coming to Dubai for some two years and he had developed a strong love-hate relationship with the country. He loved its diversity, he loved its fast moving and courageous development, he loved its people's language and culture. He hated its rabid and ugly consumerism, its ineffable hypocrisy, its unkind treatment of women and its wealth generated racism.

One day, sitting in his hotel foyer, he saw a vision walking towards him. She was a British psychologist younger than his youngest daughter. She joined him. They talked literature. They laughed a great deal. They held hands. They kissed. And became one for life. A Groundhog life. All three days of it.

But falling in love was not the big event. Apart from anything else, Parker was a one woman man despite his sixties' predilections.

The big event was a rainy day in an oasis. Parker stood in the middle of a clump of trees. As the rain increased, he spread his arms out and looked up.

The rain soaked his face and hair. He laughed and danced. For then, he had touched the face of God who had died in 1966 after spending almost two thousand years brain washing innocents. Parker was ecstatic.

And he engaged, as was his wont, in all kinds of imaginary conversations with this defunct God. Endless discussions. Why did my mother die? Why did I get sexually abused? Why was my father so cruel? Why did I fail at school? Why was I shot? Why was I arrested and tortured for my thoughts? Why did I marry bitches? Why have I never been loved for me? Answer me that Mr. Clever Dick. Hmm? Ah I thought so. You are speechless. You may well cry. Crocodile tears my friend.

He also engaged in endless imaginary discussions with everyone – including himself.

"Eh bien monsieur le président, le bon Dieu est mort en 1966?"[3]

"Bah! Monsieur l'inspecteur. Moi je n'en sais rien…"[4]

Ah! But of course monsieur le président. You are a French inspecteur génèral. You could not pronounce God dead in 1966 unless the Paris Parliament had

---

[3] "So Mr. President, the good lord died in 1966?"
[4] "Ah! Mr. Inspector. I wouldn't know anything…"

sanctioned it, the Elysées Palace had signed it and le ministère of this and that had rolled it out.

Whereas I, being British, can pronounce what I damn well like. Ah! There is true libertè for you, monsieur le président.

And mine is the God of good deeds and of love. And not that arbitrary and vengeful one that gives me Hobson's choice. But then monsieur le président, Jesus Christ was a damn good leader. A great Marxist whose political and economic philosophy was divine. Ha ha monsieur le président, a good pun that, n'est-ce pas? One drop of His blood. Just one. For, monsieur le président. I suffer so. I carry so much. I ache so deeply. Sixty years' worth of scars, monsieur le président. And all the British psychologists in the world would not break me free. Laughter is now dry, monsieur le président. My hotel in Dubai would make a fortune if it introduced the post of a self harm manager. There is a niche in the market, monsieur le président.

And the secret of the universe? It was not 42, monsieur le président. It was 518. Can't you see? Are you blind?

And the lunch break arrived.

Armed with two Palmiers, Parker sauntered into the playground. A little thin fair girl sat on the step alone and immediately attracted his attention. He walked towards her. A teacher touched him gently on the arm.

"C'est Amélia, monsieur l'inspecteur. Elle vient de nous joindre.[5] She does not speak..."

Parker walked up to Amélia and crouched before her.

"Bonjour Amélia..." he whispered quietly.

She stared at him with her beautiful piercing blue eyes. There was little life in them. Her whole face remained impassive. Not a flicker of recognition.

Parker took his jacket off. He sat to her left and the two stared ahead. She clumsily munched on a cheese sandwich whilst he greedily chomped on his second Palmier. As he bolted the last large morsel he sighed with deep regret.

Amélia ate so slowly. She nibbled around the edge of her sandwich.

"C'est bon?"[6] asked Parker ingratiatingly.

---

[5]   "This is Amélia, Mr. inspector. She has just joined us."
[6]   "Is it good?"

She ignored him and continued to nibble quietly.

"Amélia?"

Nothing.

He tore an Evidence Recording Form off a thick pad. He folded the page over and over and over. And, then, with a sharp pull, produced a sail boat. He stood the small sail boat before the little girl. He made a second one and did the same with it. A few minutes later there were seven or eight sail boats lined up in front of her.

"Pour toi, Amélia..."[7]

She stopped eating. He waited for more response.

"Tu les aimes ces bateaux?..."[8] he asked holding up the latest and largest.

She looked quickly and then went back to her cheese sandwich. Parker clumsily tore at another Evidence Recording Form and made an aeroplane. On its side

---

[7]   "For you, Amélia…"
[8]   "Do you like these boats?"

appeared the logo, 'Dubai School Inspection Bureau'. He placed the aeroplane on his head.

"Regardes Amélia..."[9]

There was a flicker of a smile.

He bent his head forward and the aeroplane crashed on to the boats.

The flicker of a smile became a little more permanent.

"Oh la la! Un accident!" Parker quickly folded another Form and made what looked like a van. He simulated an emergency siren and drove the car to the accident.

"Ah ha! Sauve qui peut!"[10] he shouted. "Allons y tout le monde!"[11] and his fingers drummed our the sound of galloping feet.

She stared at him for a long time.

---

9   "Look Amélia…"
10   "Oh! Save yourselves…"
11   "Come on everybody".

Suddenly, she broke her sandwich in half and extended a saliva sodden piece to him.

"Pour moi?"[12] he asked quietly.

She gently nodded – almost imperceptibly.

He took it. They sat eating their portion and quietly comparing bites of each piece.

"Alors, ce bon?" he asked quietly.

No reply came.

He whispered, "Merci Amélia. Ce sandwich est bon..."[13]

No acknowledgement.

Suddenly, he was filled with an overwhelming anger. He bolted his last piece and looked up. He whispered fiercely.

---

[12]   "For me?"
[13]   "Thank you, Amélia. This sandwich is good..."

"What is it with you? Why do you do this?"

And adopting a sarcastic tone he whispered fiercely, "Oh! I died on the cross so that you shall be saved! Oh yes? Then why have you forsaken me? Bloody hypocrite!"

He held his head low and his quiet voice choked.

"What about little Amélia? Why have you forsaken her? Is this your Grace you selfish self centred deity? Are you listening? What about me? Sixty years of abuse and hatred and bitterness. Never a moment of unconditional love."

He looked down at Amélia rearranging the boats and realised that his eyes were full of tears. He fought the urge to sob. His tears floated down his cheeks.

Amélia looked at him. She stood up. She moved to stand before him. Her face was level with his.

Her little hands came up and touched his wet cheeks.

He smiled and mumbled something about sand in his eyes. He could not speak as his bottom lip trembled.

Amélia came forward and put her little arms around him.

He held her gently.

"Ne pleurez pas monsieur... Don't cry..." she whispered huskily.

And he felt her gentle words cleanse sixty years of abuse and hatred and bitterness.

They embraced peacefully.

And God was reborn in this child. Parker wiped his eyes. And he was in a place with Light.

Adieu Jean Paul Sartre.

Lord?

The Dabawis and the Shargawis   **Faysal Mikdadi**

Learning on the Mount

Drag. Drag. Drag. Tradition bound and faith chained. Drag one foot after the other. Pulling a huge cart full of mendacity and hypocrisy. Shuffle that foot up a small step. Salute. Shake hands. Explain the purpose of the visit.

No one is listening.

And those rocky mountains. They conjure an image of blissful solitude. Of gentle remonstrations. Of a figure in white, arms outstretched to receive the helpless and the tired and the oppressed. And oppress them even more with two thousand years of lies and cruelties in His name.

And no one is listening.

Walking around the school where all is colour tinged with sparkling ignorance.

Young faces look up and try to smile without showing it. Crushed by the spirit of a malevolent and interfering God.

A speech about how to educate Muslims. Crush them. Turn them into soldiers for the Lord. The entire speech comes straight out of David Hunt's Satan like peddling loving hatred. And we all condemn the Muslim and praise the Christian and the Jew.

The Dabawis and the Shargawis   Faysal Mikdadi

This, sir, is an interactive board.

And this, most honoured sir, is a green environment.

Where are the trees?

There. Forty of them. One for each year of ignorance, abuse and lies. A human salad with little that is refreshing in it.

And this is the English teacher. He is from Palestine.

Jerusalem, actually.

Been here just under a year. They dragged me out of my house, touched my wife and dashed my three year old boy's brains against our garden wall. The very wall where they shot my grandfather in 1947. In the name of their God.

And this is a year ten girl. Ignorant sir. A failure. Her mother is Indian.

Ah, that explains it all.

Her eyes look up full of pain and shame and budding hatred. Bottle. Bottle. Bottle. And sharpen your teeth so that, when the cup overflows, you can bite back before their American bullet tears through your ignorant half Indian heart.

The Dabawis and the Shargawis   **Faysal Mikdadi**

There are the trees. Forty. One for each year of lies and lies and lies - forty times over. Ali Baba and the forty lies. Moses and the ten crushed hearts. Jesus Christ and the empty Sermon.

And last night, on the news, three heavily armed Israelis carry a young Palestinian man and throw him on the pavement outside his house. He is silent. His little boy stands aside not knowing if he should turn the grimace into a smile. An Israeli soldier looks at the camera and hands him a biscuit and the little boy smiles. A biscuit for two thousand years of history, a land and a life.

A good swap. It is in the Old Testament. God, who wills all, wills this. Hallelujah! Hallelujah! Praise the Lord as he sharpens His knife to murder more Palestinians.

And the forty trees?

Forty trees. Silent witnesses to all before and more to come.

The visitor stood under a tree and felt the gentle breeze on his face. He suddenly collapsed onto a bench as the English teacher droned on, not once mentioning a single student.

The half Indian girl passed by. He looked up and smiled at her. He filled his smile with as much love as a smile could hold without cracking into a sob.

Her eyes opened wide. And she stared.

He crammed more love into the smile as images of her home life streamed before him. Image by image.

Give me your tired, your poor, your huddled masses yearning to breathe free, the wretched refuse of your teeming shores. Send these, the homeless, tempest-tost to me. And I will turn them into murdering American Israeli Settlers in years to come. And Christ will be with them all. Hallelujah!

The English teacher stopped talking.

He waved her away. A few minutes of solitude and reflection.

She walked away. He was vaguely amused to note the contour of her buttocks and bottom as she walked away, covered in black from top to bottom. He dismissed her instantly.

Even sex was not desirable anymore. Dash. Dash. Dash... his little brain against the wall. God wills it.

The Dabawis and the Shargawis   **Faysal Mikdadi**

The half Indian girl stood still.

He motioned her to approach him.

She walked carefully and stood a short distance from him.

Tell me about your Arabic essay.

Her broken Arabic hid some natural talent which will never come out.

Ignorance. Ignorance. Ignorance.

Fed through and through by criminal Jews, Christians and Muslims. And their vicious God.

Who no more exists than learning, justice, humanity or decency.

And the half Indian girl's face lit up as she smiled.

A broad beautiful smile.

And she was one of the blessed. By whom. He no longer knew. But she was blessed.

And in Washington, Politicians *come and go talking of Michelangelo*. And in Palestine, more prepare to die because God, who does not exist, wills it.

The mountain range undulated nakedly but so beautifully.

To climb. Now.

The driver drove up the mountain side.

On the Mount. No White robe. No comforting words.

Clean air. Below, every ounce of injustice has enveloped the city in dirt, lies and double dealing. Each particle obscuring the past and the future. And leaving the stage set for more inhumanity.

Because God no longer exists. Can not exist.

As rivers of Palestinian blood flow down the very Mount where He never was.

And the half Indian girl?

She died long ago. Like her God.

Satanic faiths, Hunt, the intellectual murderer, calls them. Little knowing that his faith is Satan's syphilitic horn.

Undabadingy

"Good morning Salazar. How are you this fine and wonderful morning my friend?"

"Fine doctor. You are happy?"

"Of course I am. Fine cool day, beautiful trees and good health. What more could we ask for, hey Salazar my friend? Undabadingy. Undabadingy."

"What mean Unda...?"

"Undabadingy?"

"Undabadee..."

"No. No. No. Unda - baa - din - ghee. Easy. Undabadingy. Undabadingy. Easy. You try it."

"Unda - baa - din - ghee?"

"Perfect. Perfect. We'll make a flower girl of you yet!!"

"Girl? I no girl! I Salazar man..."

He drove impassively and silently for a while.

"Doctor?"

"Yes, Salazar, my friend?"

"What Undabadingy?"

"Ah! Undabadingy is it. Everything. It is the secret of the Universe. The meaning of life. The *Uqbar. Orbis. Tlon.* It is everything. You say Undabadingy and all your troubles evaporate. All is perfect after an Undabadingy."

"Salazar not understood. Undabadingy make good?"

"Perfect! You have understood!"

"Who understandings?"

"You. Salazar. Salazar understandings."

"Ah! Good. Doctor speak like Salazar. Salazar understandings."

"Ye-ees. You are a major loon Salazar my friend. Stop the car. Over there. That Lebanese coffeeshop. That's it. Excellent parking manoeuvre Salazar my friend. Now, let's go for a coffee. This way. Come. Come. Stop staring at me a if I have asked you to fly to the moon with me. Let us jump out of the car and go for a coffee and shout

Undabadingy over and over again. There. Let us sit here and tell stories of times gone by and of times to come, of events that have happened and of dreams to be, of women Undabadingied and of ones that are the stuff that dreams are made of. Let us, my friend, each wish for one thing - now. This minute. Undabadingy. Undabadingy. Undabadingy. There I have said it thrice. Go."

"Rice? Basmati or plain?"

"As plain as that girl I Undabadingied in 1963 in Shtoura whilst my father drank lemonade and talked bollocks... That was an Undabadingy and a half, Salazar my friend. What do you wish for? Name it and we will Undabadingy it magically with the sorcerer's art of materialisation and transubstantiation of the something out of nothing - like a diminutive weenie growing apace out of one thought...Choose! Two coffees. Americano please. With milk Salazar old friend? One with and one without. Pronto. Pronto. We are busily Undabadingying our world here. *Avaunt sirrah*. Ah! *I took you for a joint stool* my lord. Choose!"

"What doctor choose?"

"I go first? Okay. I shall model the art of Undabadingying to you my little jaundiced friend... Let me see. This very minute I Undabadingy being at my desk at home, my favourite novel oped afore me upon my desk (you will, dear friend, forgive my archaic English – it is for atmosphere only, of course), my eyes surveying the undulating winter trees, my ears listening to the susurration of their few leaves, imbibing a cup of home brewed tea and smiling at the benign soul mate who, by now, would have decamped because I would have given her a headache... And you? Choose? Undabadingy to you..."

"My work. I stay my work..."

Silence. Silence. Silence.

"Salazar, you humble me. I bow before you. Undabadingy will resolve it. Undabadingy will *knit up the ravelled sleeve of care. Life's but a walking shadow* dream and when you wake, you enter *the brave new world* of Undabadingy."

"Thank you doctor."

And I promise you my friend. You will keep your job. Leave it to me. You will be told soon that your contract termination is laid aside and that you can stay on. That, Salazar, is my personal promise to you before I head home to the desk, the favourite novel, the trees and the lady in red.

Undabadingy to you my dear friend.

"Thank you for the coffee. Thank you. May our dreams come true my friend. Please pick me up at four twenty this afternoon. Not four nineteen which is a disastrous waste of working hours and not at four twenty one which is discourteous - but at four twenty. Thank you for the coffee. Thank you. Thank you."

"Undabadingy doctor. Undabadingy."

"And Undabadingy to you too my dear friend. Undabadingy to you. Undabadingy... Tra la la la... Good day to you. Good day. Anon. Anon. *Tomorrow and tomorrow and tomorrow creeps in this petty pace from day to day to the last syllable of recorded time...* Undabadingy!"

Beethoven's Oasis

It was always the same. A gentle distant world of trees and green fields and quiet contentment.

What more could he ask for?

That is the word: contentment. Said over and over again, it was a mantra. One to believe in and hold close to his chest.

Contentment.

The feeling that all was well with the world. All immutable. All silent – except for the singing of the gentle wind through the trees.

His brother had gone to Scotland to hear the wind in the trees before he died. And the brother died ten days later whilst he held his infected hand and moistened it with his angry tears.

The opening of Beethoven's *Fifth* has been called 'destiny knocking on the door'. What that meant was not evident to the man standing in the middle of a clutch of palm trees. All he knew was that he loved Beethoven's *Fifth* and thought it crude, vulgar, bourgeois and common. It was the prostitute of great music. And he appreciated that this was a dream anyhow and he would not have to pay for this particular ageless prostitute.

Cloudy and misted with the fragrance of rain on sand, the oasis looked dark green. For the first time in his life, he understood why *The Holy Qur'an* described Paradise in terms of greenery, water, life, plenty and serenity. This was a little paradise and *nor was he out of it. He had just seen the face of God.* Unlike the fallen angel, he was not deprived of heaven and did not *suffer the torments of ten thousand hells.* Not yet anyhow. That, he believed, was in his hands and his hands alone. He knew that one drop of Christ's blood would save him if he said it early enough. But he did not believe.

Oh for those interminable moments of bliss. Of noisy thundering silence. Of the sheer beating heart of love. If only. And he looked around at the beautiful oasis.

He sat up in bed wide awake. It was dark. This was England. Not Dubai. He peered into the darkness and saw nothing. He could hear his beautiful wife's gentle breathing. As his eyes began to get accustomed to the dark, his wife turned over and moaned gently.

"Shshsh... Go back to sleep..." He bent down and sensitively kissed her cheek.

"Can't you sleep?" She asked sleepily.

"Just a dream... That's all..."

"Not another nightmare? Oh! Little darling. You're safe. I'll always be there... No one will ever hurt you again... No one...These are but dreams and not your little beautiful kingdom. Sleep. Sleep. My little love."

"I know... Shshsh... Go back to sleep..."

"Do you need..." she began.

"No! No!" He answered urgently.

"You're impatient. Is there something wrong?"

"A dream. Just a dream. Get some sleep. I'll have a little drink".

She turned over again whispering "Love you the mostest in the whole wide world... More than the mountains and the seas. More than the oceans and the skies. See. I win. Night night. Wake me up if those nasty dreams come again. How dare anyone upset you? You're special and if anyone upsets you I will do such things, *what they will be, I do not know, but they will be the terrors of the earth...*"

He smiled to hear her talk. Even in her half sleep, in her hypnagogic state, she spoke like William Shakespeare. His little brilliant and cultured English rose that fits every garden and is loved by every tree. Her mind opened like a rose and poured forth a fragrance beyond reality.

As he sat at the kitchen table clutching his mug of hot tea, he reflected on the fact that this was not a nightmare. The usual terrifying nightmares that haunted his life so far. This was beautiful. He could not understand why he woke up in such a cold sweat.

He suddenly realised that he was naked and very cold. His clamminess had dried into a frozen sensation. He looked at the temperature. Below zero. And the heating was off. His wife was severely asthmatic and could not breathe comfortably with the central heating on. So they slept with all heating off. And her feet were like ice against his naked body. He spent half his nights warming her up by holding her feet between his legs. They had joked that this freezing treatment should help with contraception.

The Dabawis and the Shargawis   **Faysal Mikdadi**

She had joked about them liking oral intercourse. They talked about it all the time. Her laugh was always delightful when the joke was naughty.

He got up and walked into the library where he kept his favourite blanket. A warm and fuzzy Scottish landscape that he loved so – like all things from Scotland. His first wife had given it to him when they lived in Edinburgh – the most supremely civilised city on earth. She had said that it would keep them warm after they had made love on the library floor. She used to joke that it was better in there. His books make him even harder, she said with her gentle mischievous smile and gleaming eyes. And how ugly he thought her now. What a world of topsy turvey facts.

As he bent to pick the blanket up, he realised that his first wife was right. He wrapped himself up ignoring the fire in his belly. He mused to think of its provenance. A dream of a few trees. He laughed at his trees and thought of how she had said that she did not want to know what he did with his trees.

He thought of the dream. Of Dubai. And he was filled with satisfied warmth. How he hated that society and how it warmed his very being. What a world this was! Full of little delightful and hateful contradictions.

Life was perfect with the *Fifth*, anyhow? Why an oasis? Why the dream?

He knew why. His was a loving heart and his soul had been endlessly seeking its mate. Fractured since Edinburgh. And refusing to heal.

Life was good.

But Beethoven's *Sixth* was infinitely better. Much more in tune with his special trees. Each and every one a symphony on its own. His second wife played it when they had made love in the kitchen. She said that it calmed him down and it was over quickly and then she could get on with the bloody cooking. And she did not like his excitement and said that it was not decent. As she lit another cigarette with the stub of the last one and sipped her gin and tonic. He had cigarette burns on his thighs. They spent a week in New York and he planned ways of pushing her off the World Trade Centre. She wanted to have sex in the Statue of Liberty and he refused which shocked her. And for two years after divorcing her, he could not listen to the *Sixth*. And, one day, he heard it on *Classic FM* as he drove to Gloucester on a dark January morning. He had parked his car in a lay by and sobbed his little heart out. He was found by a police squad car and two officers sat quietly with him while he cried. Then they wished him well and drove away. It had reminded him of that other brush with the law when a police car had hailed him down for driving erratically. He smiled to think of how he had replayed that piece of Mozart's and uproariously challenged the police officer to drive in a straight line with it playing in the background. She had laughed and agreed with him. She had given him a verbal caution and sent him on his way with her best wishes.

"Listen to the Brandenburg!" She had shouted as she drove off. Cultured officer. But then she was right. That wonderfully civilised European piece required one way only: a straight line. And he abhorred straight lines. Nothing like a gentle curve in life. And he stopped the car, jumped out and asked her to have dinner with him. She had said yes and they became lovers for a while. It failed because he could not quite manage it after his messy divorce. But she was kind and gentle and a balm to his fractured soul.

And when he arrived in Gloucester, he phoned his English rose and told her that he loved her. And she carried on talking about her school's impending OfSTED inspection as if he had said nothing.

"Did you hear me?" He had asked impatiently.

"Yes. I did. But I am terrified."

"Why?" and they were married exactly two weeks later after interminable telephone conversations and the stupid OfSTED inspection. God be blessed for OfSTED that took away her terror and opened the way for sheer ecstasy.

His English rose liked Tina Turner. He smiled to think of how they had rowed when he had threatened to insert every Tina Turner CD into the seat of illicit delights. They compromised and bought ear phones. He had declared that he would be damned if he would ever perform to that ugly and heart grinding voice. He had said that he would lose it. And his wife had laughed and said that he should listen to Turner's CDs in bed. It might stop him being at it every day like some lovesick teenager pumping hormones. He had been hurt and could not even think of making love. For a stupendously long period of some fourteen and a quarter minutes. And they laughed as they did at all their little quarrels, crossed index fingers as a sign of peace and made gentle and prolonged love with endless whispers of the unspeakable and the beautifully unmentionable.

He felt old and tired. Tired. Tired. Tired.

"Why are you tired?" She had asked.

Full of contentment and inner warmth, he could not answer the question. Because he was no longer tired when with her.

He put his ear phones on. *Eroica* opened assertively and he sat back in his favourite seat listening. His eyes grew heavy.

He did not know what the opening to Beethoven's Third was saying. He just loved it to bits. *Loved it to bits.* Al Mutanabi's lines came crashing through his memory. He felt euphoric although he despised the war like mention of horses and bravery but loved the gentle mention of writing equipment and parchments. A great invention was the book. Great invention. He laughed.

Later on he crept into bed quietly. He could still hear the symphony reverberating in his fractured soul desperately seeking its mate.

"Are you all right darling?" asked his wife.

"Fine. Fine. Get some sleep. Sorry to disturb you."

"Do you need to..." she left the rest unsaid as always.

"No. I'm all right. Get your rest."

"You're sickening for something... You're ill... You must be. That's twice you've said no since you got back from Dubai..."

"I'm fine. A little tired. That's all..."

"You've never said no before..."

"Tired. Tired. That's all. Sleep my dear. Sleep..."

"I'll always be your little dear..." she whispered as she fell asleep.

He fell asleep so quickly that he was surprised. He wanted to go back to the dream.

The oasis was exactly the same. He was watching himself. It was an aerial cinematic shot of him standing in the midst of trees. The camera twirled rather idiotically and the trees performed a circular dance. He thought that this was a typical fifties Egyptian movie shot. Wonderfully cretinous and obsessively watchable. He almost expected Omar Sharif to emerge from the desert and teach him how to be a true Arab and conquer the Ottoman fiends.

Beethoven's *Third* struck out.

And he knew that he was dreaming. So vividly.

So, on a Scottish blanket on the library floor. In the kitchen with Beethoven's *Sixth*. In the front room without Tina Turner.

"And your fourth wife?" Asked the tree. "What would she be? A Eucalyptus tree, I suppose?"

And he ignored the barbed comment with the contempt that it deserved.

She would be silent, serene and listen to their words. Their own music. Their little living bubbling warbling words. And they would laugh at the world and spit in the eye of danger. Soul mates. And the tree did nod sagely which pleased him and he wanted to shout, "I win!"

It started to rain. And the cameras stopped twirling – now it presented him, arms outstretched, welcoming the rain.

He felt the breeze against his wet skin as the water seeped through his clothes.

He phoned his wife. No answer. Of course there would not be an answer. She was sleeping and it was the middle of the night and this was a dream. He felt himself to be such a self indulgent and child like idiot. Like that adorable Suzy at HQ in Dubai. He had written a short story about her in the earthquake. Her prima donna stance was imminently forgivable because she had a heart of pure gold and a mind of tough metal. Adorable being.

He knew that it was but a dream. Did not think a talking tree strange. Nothing was strange in this *brave new world that had such people in it*. And the world was full of the oddest beings who never listened to old Ludwig or threw soup at waiters or loved his illicit immortal beloved and he had wanted to call his son Ludwig but they laughed at him and the baby's mother cried and he relented and called him Richard just to annoy his fascist father and how silly it was to fear a St Bernard dog called Beethoven in a silly American movie rather than the little deaf man called Beethoven in a silly American movie and to want to listen to all his symphonies in chronological order whilst reading Joyce and dreaming of Irish women whose hypocrisy was so beautiful and so exciting and then to fall in love with County Cork in Dubai where Catholics girls say no to booze and sex – the Lord be praised and Dubai be raised.

"You are dreaming stream of consciousness gibberish," whispered another tree.

"It is his age," said the oldest tree.

He still did not think his dream so odd. It was so vivid. Real. Something big was happening.

This was an epiphany. That was it. A wonderful life changing epiphany.

He wondered what would come of it. A new set of beliefs? A new world? A kinder, softer and gentler demeanour on the old irrational world. A better husband to his long suffering wife? The only one to smile at his idiotic unconventionalities. A gentler father? A less angry child?

And she appeared from the dense vegetation. Sedate with that slightly royal gait. Venus reborn. Suddenly, the world was exactly the same and its incredible difference recognised.

She joined him in the circle and they held hands.

And for the first time in his long life he had no words any more. Just silence. She had managed to do the impossible. Denude him of syntax.

"And thank God for that," said a malicious tree. "Blighter never stops talking."

"But that's what I love so about him. His voice. His words. And don't you dare hurt his feelings. Anyhow, you are only a silly tree. He is real."

But the tree was not listening.

And Beethoven's *Third* struck up again as the camera panned erratically everywhere.

For the first time he recognised what the opening of *Eroica* was.

"Opportunity knocking on the door…" shouted several trees stentoriously.

And he saw no parting from her in this life.

He awoke. He sat up with a start. Beethoven's notes were receding gently and slowly. It was daylight.

His wife sat on the edge of the bed holding a mug of hot tea.

"Another nightmare, sweetie?" she said as she wiped the sweat off his forehead and chest.

"No. A beautiful dream. So alive. So epiphanous."

"Is there such a word? Epiphanous?"

"There is now... I am a word craft. Words are born of me and not I of them..."
He smiled his tired and sad smile.

"Your skin is so soft... It's like a child's. It was the first thing that I noticed when
we first got together. You were so gentle. So careful of my needs. And I
thought it was perfect." She smiled broadly at him and held his hand.

"Not bad for a man of sixty..." he said cheerfully, warm in the reverberating
dream.

"Not bad? Bloody hell. I did not sleep all night... You dirty little bugger... How
many times? I thought that you would never finish. Then I thought that it was
because it was the first time. Yeah! Yeah! Little did I know that it was to be the
norm with you. Say bed and you're off!!"

"Are you complaining old girl?" he said laughing.

"No. No girl could. Not with your love. While we're at it, do you?..."

And he held her hand. "No, love..."

"Something is definitely wrong," she whispered as her bottom lip did a pretend sulk. She lifted the quilt.

"Good God! Something is wrong... I never thought that I would see the day that he has a lay in so late in the morning."

He gently pulled the quilt up to his chest and sat up to drink his tea.

"What was your dream about?"

"Beethoven and Suzanne," he answered.

"She is really lovely, isn't she? She's special to you. Write it down. I can see the signs... You will plummet into an awful depression and drive everyone berserk over Christmas. The *Black Dog* is at the door. Shoo him off. For goodness' sake, write it down love. I will make the breakfast."

"No, that's okay. I don't want to die of food poisoning before I have written it down..." he laughed as he threw the covers off. He ran towards the shower as she ran after him laughing and gently lashing him with the towel. He stood by the shower cubicle.

"Umm! More please..."

"You cheeky little bugger," she screamed as she snuggled up to his chest.

"Time to shower off the night," he declared quietly as he pushed her off gently.

Later on he sat in his favourite coffee shop in Dorchester and frantically wrote as Rachael, the redoubtable manager, shouted at the bemused young girl behind the counter, "Turn the bloody music off, get him a pot of tea and ask him to give me a cuddle when he has a break. And he doesn't pay. He can have whatever he wants. I mean it. He's my favourite customer, I love him so. He's special he is. Are you gonna write a poem about me love?"

He wrote, "Beethoven's Oasis" and underlined it neatly, tongue slightly sticking out like a child drawing his first straight line.

He sat back, breathed in deeply and added, "It was always the same. A gentle distant world of trees and green fields and quiet contentment".

The rest just poured out of him for the next seven hours.

Feedback

And so, by circulatory route taking longer than the arc of the sun's equinox journey to a different season, we came to the end of our feedback.

The Minister's number two looks impatient, bored and keen to speed up the sun's trip so that the weekend is here.

The feedback was over when he arrived. Alison and I withdrew.

Relief all around. Partly because the difficult messages had been delivered and we were in the clear. And partly because it was catatonically boring.

We walked out of the Director's office. She winked at me and I winked back. Only the blue eyed secretary saw that indiscretion and smiled joyfully at such explicit flirtation by two old people who should, by right, have utterly lost their libido by now.

Of course, no one knew that the Director and I have spent two heavenly weeks together. Every day. Every hour or so. We have become very close. And exchanged confidences that should embarrass her and place me on a flight home to the Lady in Red, who suffers the headache creating life with me - Bless. Theirs was an utterly innocent friendship between two passionate educationalists. But in the Arab world friendship between different genders is socially out of the question.

The Dabawis and the Shargawis   **Faysal Mikdadi**

As I slowly drew the door to the Director's office closed, I caught her eye and she winked again. I smiled back mischievously and made faces at her. Like two little children who had not yet been destroyed by vicious parents and an unforgiving society.

Oh well! That is tantamount to a marriage proposal. I had better get ready and tell the Lady in Red.

A wink? Ah! Kafka. Kafka. A wink. A wink. My kingdom for a wink. And yes, changing the "i" for an "a" did occur to me. And talking about bankers, where is my bloody money. Sent three days ago from all three sources and not a penny in my account. Thieving bastards. British banks. What did I expect.

I had not even noticed that Alison was volubly talking. I had not been listening to a single word that she was saying.

She followed me to my temporary office. Sitting down comfortably, she continued talking: an intelligent Flora and her Aunt expounding on all. "*There's milestones on the Dover Road*", except clever Alison is more likely to have said, in typical Wittgensteinian fashion, "*For a large class of cases - though not for all - in which we employ the word meaning it can be defined thus: the meaning of a word is its use in the language game. And the "meaning" of a name is sometimes explained by pointing to its bearer*" or some such utterly incomprehensible utterance. Somewhat like Christ's crap about not being unequally yoked. And people actually believe this illogic. Even when it destroys their lives.

"Ha ha ha! Jenny, mum and I want to marry Robert off to her daughter, little Scottie. Hilarious. Ha ha ha."

And, sure enough, three years later, they did. Sans love, sans means, sans future. And the Lord said so. Straight into a life of misery. Utter submission. And they attack that other submission called Islam...

And in years to come there will be much toing and froing, telephoning and wiring, travelling and flying, discussing what went wrong. As if life were a throw of the dice and had nothing to do with responsibility and choice. Because God said...

Just for once, God and your precious Son so sacrificed, shut up and let us be. Go play the prima donna in another universe and we will take our chances without your deceit, hypocrisy and lies.

We walked downstairs to the lobby. I was desperate to get rid of Alison. But she was oblivious.

"And would you believe it? Muslims arrange marriages? What savages..."

I thought of thousands of Iranians who woke up this morning feeling good to be alive. In Washington and Tel Aviv the Lord's servants were planning their funerals. No need. They could be conveniently vaporised. There we are. No mess to clear up. Like the Jews in Auschwitz, except more efficient in the killing technology. With God's help.

Meanwhile, that other God was not being helpful in shunting that Australian poetic vulnerability off.

So we stood awkwardly facing each other.

"What're you doing now?" sang Matilda of Ayres Rock.

"Meeting the wretched, the dispossessed and the ignored."

And Alison explodes into loud cackling laughter that apologises for ever having existed.

A supremely intelligent woman who did not like herself. And I, I stood before her as the intelligent man who adored himself and needed nothing apart from thought, thought, thought. Which is needed to make up for the empty universe made in six days according to Jewish mythology in which incandesces ridiculous Christian infantile gibberish. Aimed at vicious fools who hate all but their Lord who Himself is utterly hateful.

"And so, you are Lebanese?" asked the huge beard passing by.

"No!" I snapped. "I am a bloody Palestinian Muslim and always will be."

"I'm not an Arab. I'm not an Arab. Arabs conquered my country. I am not an Arab."

And I, I am not an Arab. I am a Martian.

Alison walked to the technology suite. I followed obediently for she held the purse strings.

"I hear that last night's feedback was interesting..." she giggled loudly.

Interesting? To a group of Governors who would find it hard to arrange a delivery in a natal clinic full of screaming parturating women? Men who could not make a decision on how to wipe their backsides after defecating? Yes, it was interesting. And nothing will change. We will be back next year this time with the school still a failure and the Acting Principal barricaded by a group of prima donnish Governors who want her sacked for their failures.

Ah! I am an epistemological solipsist and all your words, your values, your rotten beliefs and tired prayers are empty for my language game is different to yours.

The Dabawis and the Shargawis   **Faysal Mikdadi**

"And you will come back in June, won't you?"

No my friendly spirit for I have now wrenched my Arab soul and trodden on its rotten and stinking history and embraced the Western construct where we are superior to you all. Because we have the true faith of an idiotic shepherd who lived two thousand years ago and talked utter mythological bollocks. That is why we, and only we, have a monopoly on the truth and can vaporise you with modern weaponry whilst you squat in your obscurantist fake faith and exchange social niceties.

Let us civilise you with our superior doings.

Alison walked into the Indian IT engineer's office. She giggled and cackled and asked him to send her an e-mail of a paper she held out to him. Straight request. No problem. Push of a button or two.

Twenty minutes later, the Indian is still explaining the inexplicable and the e-mail has not been sent. We are now joined by an Emirati whose resplendent beard looks false and is begging to be pulled sharply. He joins the discussion. And I wonder if either man had ever thought of taking up where Kafka left off.

Alison is looking annoyed. She constantly reminds the two men that she would like the e-mail sent with the document attached. The two men continue an arcane discussion that no one could conceivably follow. Whilst the Arab and the Indian engage in abstruse argumentations, American Jewish settlers do the Lord's work, beat the crap out of Palestinian farmers, tear their wives' dresses off and throw them off their land to start a new Settlement. And Christ claps for joy to see his daddy's nice promise being fulfilled.

Alison bent forward across the half turned Indian man, tapped the keyboard and sent the e-mail. The Indian looked shocked. The Arab asked if I was British.

"No!" I shouted. "Palestinian! Palestinian through and through."

And my friend I am joining Hamas and Islamic Jihad and Hisbollah and every Muslim organisation that seeks to liberate Palestine. And I don't need your or the West's permission to fight for my country. If I were French, I would be a hero of the Resistance! If I were British, I would be the great behind enemy lines SAS hero. If I were American, I would be a patriot. But I am Palestinian, so I am a terrorist. To hell with you and your Christ.

Alison walked out and I followed her. She stood by her car.

"Will you be coming over?"

"I have interviews to conduct..."

"Please. Please. I am so interested to hear what you have to say..."

About what my friend? About our land and our kings and history? Jerusalem? Karameh and Deir Yassin? Where mangled Palestinian bodies were burnt as an offering to the great vindictive and vicious Lord?

"Please come..." She looked so vulnerable and so little with her tooth pick arms and her minute frame.

"Don't tell me you haven't noticed her bazookas?" had asked my Canadian colleague.

So I looked and nothing did I see: but a brilliant little girl seeking to be accepted for herself.

"I would be delighted Alison..." You could fall in love with such a sharp brain.

She backed out of her parking space and drove back in again. She backed out a second time, waved like a child and drove off in her huge purring Lexus.

I flipped the mobile and quickly dialled the number. It rang. Silence was my answer.

"Salazar? Good to speak to you. If this is called speaking! Please pick me up at two thirty. Not a minute before and not a minute after. We are British, don't you know... See you later. Bye bye."

As I put the phone away I wondered if Salazar had got the message since I heard nothing on the other end. Except his breathing - I think. I did not know that little yellow people breathed. A little like us. Amazing really what the Lord has created. Isn't it?

The Dabawis and the Shargawis   **Faysal Mikdadi**

Walking the Distance

"It's hardly believable that less than three hours ago I was a different person," he mused as he walked the three hundred or so yards to his next appointment.

Three hours. Three little hours. And he had grown so much. Although he was already sixty four and somewhat tired of growing.

The day started with his arrival at the Foundation ten minutes before the appointed time. Seven twenty. Punctilious to a tee was our stodgy and inflexible little man.

A Palestinian by birth, he had lived in England for almost half a century. And like all neophytes, he had become more British than the Queen - minus the Christian racism, of course. And he had fallen in love with Ras Al Khaimah.

He sat in the Conference Room reading Calvert W. Jones's research paper on *The Economic, Social, and Political Attitudes in the UAE: A Comparison of Emirati and Non-Emirati Youth in Ras al Khaimah*. He had to work hard to resist the urge of removing the unnecessary comma before the connective "and". But then, the author, being from Yale, was probably an American for whom English was a foreign tongue.

He spent an hour reading the research. It was the usual Western and Christian orientalism and racism with a few delicious nuggets of truth. The main truth was that the Arabs were useless citizens. He had no quarrel with this accurate finding. He had spent his whole life pretending not to be Arab. He had a dear friend who spoke, walked, thought and dialogued like an Arab but who expended huge effort denying her Arab background. And, he agreed with her since he had done precisely the same all his life.

He left the Foundation one hour late. He felt surprised that there was no irritation as there usually would be. He was beginning to adopt the local attitude of fatalism, "Ah! What can we do? What can we do?" This is always said as if one's life is entirely run by agents other than one's free self - free to choose its destiny without the interference of non existent Gods invented by frightened fools to control even more frightened fools.

He was driven to the girls' school. His driver, in broken English interspersed with endless grunts, silences and interminable indrawings of breath, explained that he would be across the road for his English lessons.

"You need them my friend," thought the hapless visitor who could not understand a word.

He walked away from the car. The driver ran after him explaining that it would be best to call the Foundation and ask for another car to take him to the next school.

"Boring wait doctor you know."

"No problem. You go to your English school and I will be fine in the girl's school."

"Girls? Where girls doctor?"

"In there," answered the doctor, his tone rising slightly as often is the case with good old racist Britons.

"There? Where? Girls? What is?"

The doctor was utterly lost. "You know girls. With little vaginas..."

"Ah! Doctor why you not say?"

You would understand the word "vagina" - mind you, the anatomical gesture was universal.

"Ha ha doctor. I like vagina."

"My dear fellow. I am rather partial to them myself you know. Usually pickled."

"Puckled? What is puckled?"

"Like a gherkin... a cucumber..."

"Ha ha! Very good doctor. Cucumber. Not called that... Ha ha ha!"

"Yes. Well, good bye."

"Doctor have good day."

"And Salazar have good day, nicky wookey?"

"Wookey nicky doctor!"

And the doctor walked into the girls' school utterly satisfied by his teaching of English as an Additional Language skills!

The school was somewhat decrepit. To the doctor, its oddness was paralleled only by the spectacular oddness of the headteacher who received him as she precipitously covered her entire face. Thank God for small mercies. All through his visit, the Hijab slipped upwards and covered the head's eyes and she regularly pulled it down. The gesture reminded him of a colleague who constantly pushed his glasses up on his nose. And like him, she stopped talking when she did that gesture. Like shutting eyes when sneezing or stopping talking when farting. One thing at a time.

"Welcome. Welcome. Honoured doctor. You are our teacher. You are our benefactor. And may the Lord give you strength..."

The Dabawis and the Shargawis   **Faysal Mikdadi**

The doctor stopped listening, hoping that this hypocritical preamble would be cut short. Women came and went, their faces covered. He asked his questions and felt odd talking to just two eyes. The head's hands were much older than her beautiful eyes.

"See! Even when we are covered up, as a man, you look for attributes of beauty and, by implication, of sexuality. You sexualise us utterly," he remembered Shirin saying in 1964.

"Never!" he asserted vigorously, as he took a nipple in his mouth and she moaned. He loved the way she started moaning so quickly. All the quicker to get to his core!

The women's answers were utterly without use. They were polite platitudes that gave no opinion. All at the Education Zone was perfect.

Coffee was drunk. Sweet was munched. More inanities were uttered and he found himself staring at an empty note book.

He asked for two students' files: Fatma and Aisha - he intoned the names as he frantically shuffled pages as if searching for the names.

A woman ran out (running being simply not shuffling).

The Dabawis and the Shargawis   **Faysal Mikdadi**

He sat back and read the two records. Quite impressive. He wrote a few notes, got up and bid all adieu.

The head jumped up and said, "Afore you go," (how else would one represent that wonderfully arcane Classical Arabic?) "Afore you go, you must meet the nurse..."

They walked down the corridor to the infirmary where they were met by an Egyptian nurse. And the doctor was desperate to faint. Suffer a heart attack. Anything to be resuscitated by those luscious lips.

"See! You can't even see us as a profession..."

He stepped out of the school and remembered that he no longer had a car.

He approached a huge man sitting idly by a tree. He asked him how to get to the boys' school.

"Are you an Arab?"

"No. I am a Palestinian."

The man stared at him, got up and embraced him hard.

"I am a Syrian... We're both finished... Come. I will give you a lift."

They walked out onto the road. There were no cars. Just one huge American style school bus.

"This way please doctor."

And they mounted the bus. He sat in the row behind the driver and they set off.

"I come from Aleppo. I went to visit for a week. I left here one man. I came back a week later another man. I stayed with my mother. Ancient woman may He keep her for me to love. I saw what I would never want to see. I went to the mosque. We prayed. The army arrived. Every man in a white Jalabiyah was taken out. The officer said that two men in white Jalabiyahs had attacked a police station. They took the men - thirty of them. They walked them to the playground. And we heard. Ta ta ta ta ta ta. They shot 'em all. A digger came and picked them up one by one and threw them in a huge hole in the ground. They covered them and we went home for lunch. I couldn't eat. It reminded me of 1981. Our prison was full. More prisoners arrived. They took a thousand and told them to leave. It was desert out there. But the men ran - so joyful to be free. Ta ta ta ta ta ta ta. Every single one of them. Left there to bake in the sun to be cooked meat for jackals and vultures. The Jews do the same to your people I know. Here is your school. Boys' school. Why do they bother. They'll kill them all one day. And if they don't. Israeli and American tanks would roll in and finish the job."

They shook hands and the doctor stood in the sun watching the bus kicking up a huge amount of dust.

"And you are?" asked the corpulent principal.

The doctor introduced himself and said that he was confident that the principal would have been informed of his visit.

"I've been informed of precisely nothing. But what's new. What do you want?"

Research. His Highness. Foundation.

"Led by a woman..." intoned the principal.

Research. Educational Zone.

"Led by another woman..." said with the same impassive face.

Fact finding. Report. His Highness. Just in case it was not heard before. And it obviously wasn't.

"His Highness is our distinguished father and our lighthouse. Without him our ship would flounder on the rocks..."

The Dabawis and the Shargawis   **Faysal Mikdadi**

And the doctor stopped listening.

"So you want to know about the Educational Zone run by a woman. It is a great day in our nation. It is the first time that a woman has been appointed to such a high post. I tell my wife that my boss is a woman. And how she laughs. She thinks I mean her. A woman. I wish her every success. I hope that this works for our nation. A woman has her troubles of course. But, in today's world... I have three daughters. Two doctors and one educationally backwards. I love them all equally. The most successful is my pretty little one who failed at school. Married. Two boys. Beautiful. I am so proud of the doctors. I tell my wife that we have no worry on health grounds. Two doctors in the family. I think that women should be given a chance. Women into leadership. You Lebanese?"

"No. Palestinian."

"Ah! Leyla Khaldi! Hanan Ashrawi! Great Palestinian success stories. Yes women are great. Have a daughter?"

Yes. A beautiful girl. Catherine.

"Not Palestinian name that I know of... Boys?"

One intelligent boy. ("See! See! The girl is beautiful and the boy is intelligent...")

Successful boy. Richard.

"Richard? As in the Lionheart?" Thunderous silence. "Of the Crusades?"

Richard Darwish.

"Darwish? Darwish? Wonderful. Wonderful. Let me shake you by the hand. And I would like to give you this book of poetry. Arabic poetry. And this notebook with beautiful local pictures. And this book of English grammar. You must keep on top of your English or you will lose it... And the Educational Zone. Awful communications. Useless service. Bad training sessions. Never answer the phone. People have no professional pride in what they do. There we are. There is your report. Other than that, all is well with Educational Zone..."

Thank you. Thank you. Thank you.

And the doctor walked out of the school and started the short walk of a few hundred yards.

A car stopped and offered him a lift. He declined saying that he liked walking.

He walked on reflecting on the morning.

Three hours. Three hours. That was all.

"Syria. I left here one man. I came back a week later another man."

Three hours. And the doctor left the Foundation one man and came back three hours later another man.

He woke up British.

He walked back an Arab. From Palestine. And Syria. And Ras Al Khaimah. And Dorchester. And Dorset. And Beirut.

And everywhere and nowhere.

The Dabawis and the Shargawis   **Faysal Mikdadi**

Joy in Dubai

Joy held a British passport. Joy was born and brought up in Dubai. Saïd[14] held a United Arab Emirates passport. Saïd was born and brought up in Britain. The two had became acquainted at work in Dubai. Saïd had been visiting regularly for some two years for short periods of two to three weeks at a time. The work had been relentless. But the money was good. Joy worked in the same building. That was how they met. Over the regular visits, they got to know each other well. They became very close friends. In fact, to the unpractised eye they would have looked like any other couple madly in love. Would have, except that Saïd was an irritable and impatient old man with the emotional age of a two year old. Joy was a beautiful and gentle young woman with a maturity much older than Saïd's. He could no more fall in love with Joy than he could paraglide without help. He was set in his ways. He worked hard. And every night, at ten o'clock, he phoned home to talk to his wife. Everyone around him thought that habit so touching. It was rare to see an old man still in love with his wife. It was obvious that Saïd was besotted with his little pretty wife to whom he was devoted. Everyone could see that he was lost without her and missed her desperately. Like a child without his mother on his first day at school.

---

14   Saïd is Arabic for 'happy'.

The Dabawis and the Shargawis   Faysal Mikdadi

Joy could no more fall in love with Saïd than she could sun bathe naked on a Dubai beach. Where Saïd was reaching the end of his career, she was at the starting line. Where Saïd saw books, gardening and a quiet life before him, she saw the hustle and bustle of the battle of life, which she fought vigorously and intelligently. But she did admire him and wanted so much to have his good opinion of her. She worked hard to be worthy of his demanding friendship.

They became trusting friends. He helped her with his infinite experience of the place of work. She helped him accommodate to the more conservative pace of life in a Muslim society. He made her laugh with his old man's irreverence and age old indifference to anything vaguely socially determined. She laughed with a great sense of liberation for never had she been given the freedom to laugh at her host country's traditions.

Saïd was also politically, socially and morally an absolute maverick. Joy was the product of her conservative society. He rebelled at everything like the overgrown adolescent he used to be some forty five years ago. She, through tortuous experience, had learnt to accommodate every social norm, every tradition and every outdated religious demand.

Whenever Saïd visited Dubai, they spent every free minute together or with other work colleagues. With Saïd's infectious lunacy, they all laughed at every single minute of their lives and jogged along their working lives naturally, carefully imitating ducks taking to water. Because of that, Saïd had become very popular at work.

Joy's life had little joy in it. Saïd's life had a great deal of contented happiness in it. Joy had learnt to conform. Saïd had created a cocoon around him to protect himself from any social harm. The only thing that mattered in his life was his novels and his poetry. All else was at best an irrelevance and at worst a damn nuisance and necessary evil. His wife smiled tolerantly and let him be as long as he behaved himself. She always felt that he had many other compensating character traits.

Joy and Saïd spent hours walking by the beach, talking in coffee shops and sitting in restaurants eating little and telling each other stories. They got to know each other very well. Joy opened her heart out to Saïd and told him about her upbringing. She took him to al Ain and showed him where she used to live, her schools and everything that meant anything to her in that delightful and green town. He, on the other hand, told her about his life as a child in various Arab countries before his parents moved him to Britain and boarding school. He told her about his mother's death when he was six, about his father's Victorian strictures, about his abusive teachers and about fagging for cruel and pompous sixth formers. He told her about the awful sexual abuse he was subjected to as a child in his boarding school. How he had failed and how he had attempted suicide. He told her how his beautiful wife had somehow saved him. His stories were moving and endless.

After a while, there was virtually nothing that they did not know about each other. They had become true soul mates.

One Friday, they met for coffee at their favourite coffee shop 'Chez Paul'. The strong black coffee was so good. The croissants were delicious. The brioches were to die for. And the laughter was infectious. They sat there for four hours talking away cheerfully. Every now and then Saïd would rush out of the coffee shop and come back with news that new thyme pizzas had arrived or that new hot croissants had come out of the oven. And then a feast would start with much utterly unnecessary eating. And it must be said that both Joy and Saïd did not really need to eat. In fact it could be said that if they had both desisted from eating for, say a week or two, the benefit to their waist lines would be quite considerable. But the sheer joy of being alive at such tender young ages made them utterly indifferent to any such social nonsense. In the case of Joy, youth was a reality. For Saïd, it was borrowed happily from her lovely smile and gentle character.

"Conference!" shouted Saïd.

"Shshshsh! Not so loud, Saïd," whispered Joy, her eyes roaming all over the coffee shop to make sure no one has heard his loud stentorian declaiming voice.

"Why?" he whispered as loudly as he could do with his usual mischievous smile and very naughty eyes that, to Joy, were growing bigger every day.

"You don't shout like that here..."

"Why?"

"Well, it's just not done..."

"Says who?"

"Whom, I think you will find..."

"Bollocks..." he shouted cheerfully.

"Saïd, please!!"

"Sorry old bean. Did not mean to use a bad word. As for their society, well I have six letters making up two words. Now, the first word starts with the letter 'f'. It ends with the letter 'k'. In the middle it has the first letter of the UAE followed by 'c'. The second word is 'it'. Voilà. I rest my case, milord."

They both laughed.

"Anyhow, Saïd. You called a conference. What do you want a conference about?"

"We should hold an extremely lengthy discussion on what we should buy Susan as a present from Dubbidubbido. What think you, old bean?"

"Does she like jewellery?"

"Does the Pope like Mass?"

"What about a ring?"

"No fingers left to wear 'em on."

"What about a bracelet?"

"One more bracelet on her arm and she would keel over with the excess weight."

"Necklace?"

"Would crack her neck with the extra weight alongside the other ones bought over the last two years."

"What do you want to buy her?"

"Something very Arab. I don't know, like a good Falafel sandwich..."

"You can hardly fly home with a Falafel sandwich."

"Says who?"

"Whom, I think you will find..."

"Bollocks I think that you will find..."

"Why? Why? Oh why?"

"Why? Why? Oh why - What? if one may be so bold as to ask your most boring highness..."

"Why do you have to use such toilet language?"

"My dear Joy, whereas my dear bollocks spend a great deal of time suspended precariously over a precipice called the toilet and whilst their sole purpose appears to be to irritate one in the current extreme heat, they are not of the toilet in the sense of obscenity. They are delightful in many ways which I could enumerate for you should you desire it."

"No thank you..."

"My dear Joy, have you always been a prude or did you work at it all your life?"

"My dear Saïd, have you always been a user of the language of the gutter or did you spend your life living in one and learnt how to speak there?"

"Ooooooooooh!! Excuse me for breathing... And now, can we get back to our conference? Where were we at?"

The Dabawis and the Shargawis   **Faysal Mikdadi**

" 'At which point were we?' would be a better way of saying it, I think you'll find..."

"Says who..."

"My English teacher always said that you should not end a sentence with a preposition."

"And mine, his name is Winston Churchill, says that *this is the sort of English up with which he will not put.*"

Le mot juste was Saïd's gift.

"Conference please!"

"Okay, what would you like to buy for your wife?"

"A Falafel sandwich..."

"Oh don't start that again..."

"A Falafel sandwich..."

"I know. Why don't you get her a box of Lebanese and Arab sweets. She would like that. They're a bit pricey, but they are certainly cheaper than jewels."

"By Jove, you are a veritable genius. We will make a flower girl of you yet. Let us go. Do you know a good place?"

And the two walked cheerfully around the Mall looking for the sweet shop. They found one and walked in.

It was an Aladdin's Cave. Joy looked around quietly and examined the price tags on each box occasionally tut tutting at the sellers' exorbitant greed.

Saïd stood like a man transformed. His face lit up. He looked around from surface to surface and smiled broadly. His eyes grew wide at the treasures before him. Joy noticed for the first time how young he looked. He looked like a child as he ran from tray to tray. He started to run from one section to the other. Every time he saw some sweet he recognised he would exclaim its Arabic name loudly and clap his hands. Joy watched him run for a while.

He had reached the Lebanese section and became veritably hysterical with excitement.

"Oh look. Ma'amoul. I love those. We used to have them at home. We had to eat them without making a mess. And my father was so strict about not making a mess. How do you eat a Ma'amouli without the icing sugar falling off and the pastry flaking onto your front. Ah! Ah! Ah! Look Barazi'. I love the sesame seed on them. I like them a little overcooked. Look! Look! Knafè. With the syrup. Can I have some? Can I have some? Susan loves it. Can we have some?"

Joy stood there looking at this sixty year old man jumping from leg to leg with sheer excitement. He could hardly disguise his joy. He clapped his hands and smiled. His eyes grew even wider if that were possible.

Joy walked over to him as he held up a sweet made up of peanuts covered in crystalline sugar.

"Joy! Joy! What is this one called? I forget.... Oh.... Oh, yes. Aramish. Aramish. Aramish."

And at every word of the newly remembered name, Saïd did a little jig with overflowing excitement.

Suddenly Joy noticed that several people in the shop were looking at him quizzically and a few disapprovingly.

She walked to him and took him by the arm quite firmly.

"All right! Stop that! Now!"

"Oh, but Joy this is so lovely…" he sang out.

"Stop it. Now. That is enough. Stop it."

She almost shook him slightly as a mother might a recalcitrant child.

Suddenly, Saïd's eyes grew smaller as he knitted his brows at her.

She manoeuvred him towards the restaurant gently. They passed the Barazi' shelf and she took two boxes.

"You can buy those for Susan…"

He walked obediently.

"Would you like some Knafè?"

Saïd shook his head.

"Come on. Let's have some. It would be lovely."

He nodded without speaking.

They found a table and sat facing each other. Saïd held his head down and said nothing. The Knafè and tea arrived. They ate and drank quietly.

"Saïd?"

"Yes?" he whispered.

"I'm sorry I was abrupt. I was doing it for you. This is an oppressive society. Jumping up and down is frowned upon. I was trying to save you from any of those people showing you disrespect. That is all, old chap..."

Saïd nodded as memories of an emotionally stunted father whizzed through his brain. After his mother died, there was little joy left in their home. She had previously brought all the laughter that reverberated around the house. His father was too strict to allow any excessive show of emotion. He banned flippancy in their lives.

"Happiness is illegal in this society..." said Joy nervously as she looked at Saïd with compassion. He looked like a two year old who had lost his toy. His eyebrows met in the middle of his glowering forehead and the sides of his mouth bent downward and he looked as if he were going to burst into tears.

Joy paid for the Knafè and coffee.

"We are due at Camille's at 7.30. Would you like to go back to the hotel for a little sleep?"

Saïd nodded still glowering.

"Come, I will drive you back?"

"No," he said softly. "It is out of your way. I will take a taxi. Pick me up at seven. I will walk you to your car." He spoke authoritatively and Joy thought better than to argue.

The Dabawis and the Shargawis   **Faysal Mikdadi**

They walked to the lift and descended to the bowels of the earth. Beside the lift, he absently read a notice requesting customers kindly to dress modestly and asking couples to refrain from public shows of affection. It vaguely amused him to think of a government that asks its people not to show love. Maybe one day, there will be signs up asking people to hate each other and to do each other harm.

The lift noiselessly took them down. They walked into the car park. After some walking around in confusion, they found the car. Joy got into the driver's seat. Saïd stood aside as she cautiously backed out.

She looked out of the window and saw him waving his right hand without moving his arm, in exactly the same way that his granddaughter of one did. Joy waved back and smiled broadly. He did not smile.

As she drove off, she could see him in her rear view mirror walking towards the lifts with his head bent and his steps tired.

As she turned the corner to start the car's climb up, she had a last glimpse of him turning to get into the lobby to catch the lift.

What she did not see were the tears that streamed down his cheeks. But she knew him well enough to know that they were there.

And she cursed this society that could hurt vulnerable and gentle little children such as he was.

Lebanese Diva

The car swerved into the university car park with some screeching noise and at speed. Jane and Saif stepped out of the car as the driver jumped out making a great fuss of Saif. He held the door open for him, took his laptop and box of papers and ran into the building smiling and curtseying. Behind walked Jane laden with several bags, boxes and a large laptop. Saif tried desperately not to laugh as he attempted to help her with her load. He managed to take one bag off her. The moment he did so, the driver came rushing out and took it off him whilst utterly ignoring Jane.

The heat had already spread into every little corner. Even the shade was no protection against the searing sun. The wonderful colours of the university, its waterfalls, ponds and lush green trees appeared at odds with the extreme heat.

Saif and Jane walked in and the Pakistani President Musharaf look alike caretaker pranced towards them speaking in his high pitched voice incomprehensibly. Jane appeared to understand and fully engaged him in the morning chat. Saif immediately displayed his wonderfully inane smile that clearly declared to all and sundry that he could not understand a single word that was being said and that, if he could understand, he was not in the slightest interested in social chit chat. He envied Jane her touching ability to chat to everyone and put them so wonderfully at ease by making them feel that she was intensely interested in the minute trivia of every aspect of their inordinately dull lives.

As the lift rose to the second floor, both Jane and Saif maintained a deep silence as if saying good bye to moments of peace now lost for the rest of the working day. Their twenty or so inspector trainees may have been fully grown and experienced adults, but each and every one decided to adopt the two as their ineffable mum and dad. Their learnt helplessness was absolutely draining. Yet, both Jane and Saif had taken to playing the part of parents par excellence quite well. Indeed, they appeared vaguely to enjoy doing so. They dispensed endless advice on the self evident, explained in great detail the clearly obvious to all normal people, analysed the simplest problems and their charges wallowed in being so babied. Occasionally, Jane and Saif exchanged desperate glances when one participant was particularly helpless. Like the poor chap who so desperately missed his wife back home that he could do nothing – not even apparently dress himself in any way remotely suitable for a professional.

The two tutors walked into their conference room and quickly, efficiently and silently started preparing for the day's work. Saif connected his laptop, started the morning ritual of trying to get the technology to work only to rush off looking for President Musharaf to ask him to get him a technician to get things going.

Slowly, and infuriatingly early, the trainees started arriving. Being Dubai each man had to go up to Saif and vigorously shake hands pumping his up and down as if the fate of the world depended entirely on the possibility of dislocating it at the shoulder at every meeting. This was followed by each person taking it upon himself to ask the daily, endless series of inane questions enquiring after Saif's health, his rest the previous night, his family, his state of mind, his enjoyment of Dubai. Saif answered 'fine, thank you' to everything and was waiting for the questions to start getting more intimate by the second. The endless volleys of 'fine, thank you' were discharged like a small machine gun.

Meanwhile, each man coming in briefly turned to Jane and mumbled a greeting as if talking to a woman may be misconstrued as attempting anything remotely untoward. Occasionally, a woman walked in and completely made up for the way the men had ignored Jane by engaging her with an endless line of trivial queries, occasional hugs and some slobbering kisses.

And each morning, Saif would suddenly freeze at the sound of one particular pair of footsteps. All activity would cease and he would leave the room walking with considerable confidence towards the gents only to have a quick look at

Goddess. She walked in that wonderfully Cleopatra like manner that clearly sought to say to all and sundry, 'Don't even think about it. I am unattainable you little perv.' And like every morning, Saif would mumble a greeting from behind steamed glasses and a clunky duck walk so particular to his somewhat rotund little shape. And every morning the Goddess would go into her separate conference room where she was running her own training course.

Saif would then dejectedly shuffle back to the conference room where Jane would now be almost ready for the day.

Just like the car had swerved into the car park announcing its regal presence, so did Souzan. She waltzed into the room with her Palestinian scarf flowing behind her and fluttering like a bevy of slaves genuflecting at her every step. Her huge sun glasses rested suavely on her luxurious hair and gave the impression of an extra pair of eyes. She placed her folders and papers on the table and immediately waltzed to the air conditioning control panel and started fiddling with it as she did every morning. As she looked at it, she hunched her shoulder and wrapped her scarf around her more tightly. President Musharaf, who had been hovering about just outside, came running in and asked her if she was cold although what came out of his mouth sounded more like one long burst from a tired wind instrument.

"Cold? Cold?" shrieked Souzan.

"Yes madam..." sang the President with his head sliding from side to side in a futile attempt to ingratiate himself with the angry diva.

"Cold? Don't you understand that I live in Canada where the temperature can go down to twenty below zero? And here in Dubai I am more cold than I am in Canada where I live because I am now a Canadian."

"Madam is Canadian?" asked the President with a very wide smile that appeared even wider when his head danced from side to side.

"Yes madam is. I am a Canadian citizen..." There was no need to add anything to this as Souzan's silence was as pregnant as the executioner's eyes at the moment that the deed is done. If air could talk it would have added "I am a Canadian citizen you little silly intelligible comic sub continental cretin".

"Goodness gracious madam. I will get the technician to fix. Technician he fix. He fix air condition. Become good. No more Canadian cold madam". And President Musharaf scurried out of the room at great speed meant to convey efficiency. As soon as he turned the corner he fell into a comfortable chair and dived into deep meditation.

A few minutes later a technician came in. Saif explained that when you pressed the on button nothing happened and when you pressed the off button even less happened. The technician pressed the on button and nothing happened. He then pressed the off button and even less happened.

"Not working," he said peremptorily and walked out.

A little while later another technician came in and dived on the floor in front of the large and complex looking machine. He fiddled a little and everything started to work properly.

Saif relaxed at last. He shook the Goddess out of his mind once and for all.

"Good morning Souzan. Did you have a good evening?" Asked Saif adopting the 'I am supremely interested' expression which was akin to a horse on seeing hay.

"Oh my God! I had a night from hell. Oh God! I had to be taken to Accident and Emergency. I thought I was going to die. They gave me morphine. It was terrible. I thought I was going to die. I was taken to hospital in my husband's car. Lights on. Hooting like mad." All this was said at great speed as the scarf flew hither and thither and the glasses played up and down her forehead and eventually were severely disciplined into their place on the top of her magnificent head of hair.

"I'm sorry to hear it. You are all right now though. What happened?"

"Oh my God! You wouldn't believe it. Happened? Happened? You ask? I tell you. Incredible. I was cooking dinner. Just dinner. Nothing much. I just put my hand out to check that the hob was on. I was badly burnt. Awful. My hand almost disappeared the burns were so severe. They had to give me morphine. Here! Look!"

Souzan held her hand out for all to see. The hand was a dainty little pretty apparition with nothing at all on it apart from a large number of massive rings. Saif made a face indicative of great amazement at the absolutely nothing that he could particularly see of the hand that allegedly almost disappeared last night.

"See? See? Thank God it is better now. You should have seen it last night. They gave me morphine you know. It was awful. Morphine. I thought that I was going to die. My husband was marvellous. He took me to hospital driving incredibly fast. He went on and off pavements and people were scurrying here and there because it was a very serious accident. They gave me morphine you know."

Jane mumbled a few polite inanities that seemed to satisfy Souzan who returned to the air conditioning controls as she huffed, puffed and trembled. She pushed her collar up and glared at President Musharaf who appeared briefly, smiled inanely and ran off looking very officious.

"I like your scarf. It is a Yasser Arafat scarf, isn't it?"

"Jane!" Souzan's voice had risen several pitches and she was screeching now. "How could you use that man's name? He was a corrupt criminal who did nothing but steal from everyone. He was awful... How could you link this lovely piece of cloth to that criminal?" She held the scarf aloft, looked at it for a short while then dropped it into the bin.

"I'm not wearing it anymore."

Jane, who had formed a secret attachment to President Arafat not dissimilar to Saif's secret attachment to the Goddess, smiled and looked very busy.

"Yasser Arafat!!" spat Souzan.

The Dabawis and the Shargawis   **Faysal Mikdadi**

Saif felt that he had to say something to save the situation so he thanked Souzan for her help in interpreting English into Arabic over the course. Several inspectors gathered around to listen.

"I don't mind. I enjoy interpreting. We Canadians are naturally bilingual. I like it. Although I prefer to speak English. I am not too keen on Arabic so my daughters are not going to learn it."

One man who had been standing to the side with his hands in his pockets came forward and jutted his jaw out pugnaciously.

"A passport does not make a national identity. Your identity is what you are born into... You are Lebanese..."

Souzan's face turned a little pale. She raised her arm like someone reading a passionate poem by Byron and held forth in a loud and angry voice.

"I'm what I choose to be. The accident you call my birth does not give me my identity. You have completely misunderstood my intent. I want my daughters to be Canadians so that they can have choices in a civilised society and not be crushed by male chauvinism. They have enough studying to do without having to learn yet another language just because we are here for a short time..."

The man had replaced his hands in his pocket and adopted a more conciliatory stance. He smiled at Souzan and spoke to her softly.

"I must apologise to you for appearing to be critical. I can assure you that there was no intent to criticise. I just meant that one..."

He left the rest unsaid and was providentially saved by a sudden terrifying occurrence. It was difficult to recognise what was happening.

Saif thought that he was having some kind of slight stroke as he felt a little unsteady on his feet and thought that his brain was giving him an odd sensation of whooshing its own way away from his corporeal existence.

Jane thought that her desk had an unsteady leg or two.

The man thrust his hands deeper into his pockets and looked around with a quizzical expression on his face.

The Dabawis and the Shargawis   **Faysal Mikdadi**

Souzan quickly picked her scarf out of the bin, wrapped it around her neck and readjusted her huge sunglasses on her head and dived under the nearest table shrieking "Earthquake! Earthquake!".

The look on Saif's face indicated that he was much relieved to hear that this was only an earthquake and not a stroke. He sat down and stared at Souzan with a mixture of amusement and fascination and wondered what Goddess was like in bed and whether he should rush out and save her life by carrying her out of the building, into his car and to his bed. Meanwhile, Jane looked at him and indicated the door with her eyes. The man with his hands in his pocket shrugged his shoulders and walked back to his seat where he sat quietly awaiting the inevitable hysteria attendant on such occasions and Souzan soon fulfilled his aspirations.

"Earthquake! Earthquake!" She shrieked from under the table. "Get under the table. Quick. It is the safest option. Get under the table and adopt this position. Put your head as low as it would go. Like this. Put it between your legs..."

"...and kiss your arse goodbye," shouted Saif. Jane started laughing and Saif joined her.

Souzan's head emerged from under the table and her face started to get redder by the second. She looked left and she looked right.

"That was an earthquake. Honestly. You are supposed to get under the table..." she looked desperately embarrassed.

Saif and Jane suggested that it would be a good idea if everyone evacuated the building quietly. Both dived out of the door carrying their laptops and papers and walked downstairs onto the grassy knoll and waited for instructions to go back into the building. These never came.

Souzan joined them and volubly expounded on her experiences of endless natural disasters over the years. Jane, always the polite listener, smiled and nodded. Saif wondered what would happen if she kept nodding so regularly. Would she suddenly nod herself into a deep hypnotic sleep?

Souzan shouted into her mobile in loud and hysterical Arabic. She was speaking to her mother in Beirut telling her how she had survived an earthquake.

She was talking at great speed in the best Joycean stream of consciousness manner. Suddenly Saif realised how similar she was to a Lebanese archetype in her mannerism and almost arbitrary terminal pronouncements. It was rather like yapping incessantly with little effect on any one but the archetype herself who got exhausted.

Saif was filled with a warm and loving feeling as he realised that Souzan was worth her weight in gold. Her innate and loving kindness utterly made up for her interminable volubility. He had learnt a salutary lesson as a result of the earthquake. Every cloud had a silver lining.

Saif soon forgot all about Souzan, all about the earthquake and all about everything as the Goddess stepped out of the building.

"We survived an earthquake! We survived an earthquake!" shrieked Souzan.

As the Goddess walked towards Saif, her magnificent shape undulated in that wonderful womanly way. Saif had unashamed images of what she would look like without any clothes on and thought of something witty to say. Meanwhile, the little brain that was left functioning found a very secure home in the gorged member between his shaky legs.

"Did the earth shake for you?" he gasped in what was meant to be a hilarious witticism.

Goddess looked at him in her usual polite but awfully superior way. That way that said, "I know. I know. You can't help it. But there we are. You will be all right in your own way but not through having me. That you can be sure of..."

"It did shake indeed," she whispered in that divine voice. "Yes. It did. And I must say when it happened I couldn't believe it because at the very moment that the earth shook I was in the very process of looking at a really dishy chap. Did you see him around? He wears the national dress... Oooooh! He is something else..." And her voice took on that ultimate orgasmic quality that rendered Saif momentarily utterly ape like in every way as his tongue lolled helplessly everywhere except in his mouth.

"We survived an earthquake! We survived an earthquake!" Shrieked Souzan to no one in particular.

President Musharaf ran out of the building shouting, "Gettings out everybody. Gettings out. Earths quaking. Earth quakings... Staying out. I fixings..."

Saif and Jane walked toward their car trying hard to maintain a straight face.

"Goings home. Buggerings off," whispered Jane.

"Yeah sure!" whispered Saif. "National dress my foot. She's probably cold and unfeeling anyhow!"

Possessed

It is a truth universally acknowledged that a man passing the age of sixty years is in need of a second youth.

It has ever been thus and so does it remain.

At least that was what Dr. Sami felt that morning. A creature of habit, he had woken up at six, showered, dressed and made his way to the hotel dining room by six thirty. As he ate his unchanged morning fare, he thought of how youth was so long ago.

Being in Dubai had brought memories of his early upbringing in Beirut some half a century ago. The Arabic language, ineffable hospitality, awkward gentleness, inability to speak straight and the relentless heat brought quiet images of years back. As days went by, these images turned into moving pictures which slowly acquired colour, then noise and then real life. A little tremor evoked vivid memories of the huge earthquake in 1956. He could hear his sister singing loudly about how she could dance whilst he lay in bed crying in terror. He could see his mother running into the room, picking him up and racing out to the warm garden in the middle of night. He felt the thrill of being allowed to play in the garden in the dark.

The Dabawis and the Shargawis   **Faysal Mikdadi**

Wherever he went, Dr. Sami saw his childhood, boyhood and youth. He fancied that he met his young self in different guises and in different places.

He grew younger day by day despite the aches and pains brought on by the remorseless ageing process and unnecessary hard work. The habit of extreme and largely unproductive hard work was acquired after fifty years of living in Britain where great pride was taken in working fingers to the bone without any discernible impact on one's pocket.

And then she walked in.

A woman whose very presence awakened every little uncomprehending youthful zest for life. The pains and aches gently disappeared. Lines of magnificent poetry rose and filled his very belly with the excess of unadulterated heat. He recited them as if they were his own when they were every other man's. And the world was young again. And the dreams flooded back. And the nights were long and blissful.

Her very presence took years off his age and made him even more in tune with his youth.

The Dabawis and the Shargawis   **Faysal Mikdadi**

She was indescribable and ageless.

Dr. Sami politely carried on eating his breakfast. Swallowing was out of the question. Sweating was plentiful. Language simply disappeared. And there it was. Adolescence at its best. And when she said 'good morning' he manfully responded with an uncomprehending grunt that appeared to gurgle its way out of his deepest depth despite his best efforts at retaining some modicum of ineffable dignity as he stared at her through the embarrassingly steamed glasses which he tried to blame on the humidity in an air conditioned environment.

The day at work went by at great speed. He bubbled and laughed and chatted and danced until he headed back to the hotel exhausted.

A quick shower. A little attempt at futile beautification. A dignified walk downstairs. A taxi and he was at the restaurant where the birthday dinner was taking place.

Three pairs sat around a rectangular table. Dr. Sami sat between his colleagues Elaine and Munira. Elaine sat to his left and maintained some decorum despite her urgent desire for a cigarette which was doing her more damage than the cigarette itself eventually will. Being Ramadan, the guests sat waiting for the muezzin to call for prayer signifying that the fast may be broken. Munira sat to his right. At the top of the table next to her sat her bosom pal Alia with her husband to her right. Munira's husband sat to the right of Alia's facing Dr. Sami.

Dr. Sami felt an unreasonable urge to start eating dates against all traditions and expectations. He resisted it and occupied himself dreaming of the breakfast woman. Fortunately he was not fasting or else the fast would have been shattered with only an infinitesimal part of his impure thoughts.

He turned to Munira and started a conversation in order to fill the time until he could dive into the dish of dates laid out so temptingly before him.

"So, old girl, when was the last time you went back home?"

"To South Africa? Let me see. In 2005. I remember it so well because my baby had to be circumcised".

Feeling a little awkward at this piece of information, Dr. Sami smiled inanely to indicate that he was utterly interested in what was most uninteresting.

"Yes. I so well remember it. He didn't like it very much and said that he would never be naughty again. I remember putting his cap on and then losing it in his nappy. It was so funny."

Dr. Sami attempted a change of subject not having the foggiest idea what a cap was.

"Ah. Yes. Most interesting... And... Tell me, how is your husband getting on in his new job? Hmmm?"

Before she could answer, the waiter arrived carrying several drinks. Dr. Sami immediately asked for apricot juice which reminded him of his midnight suhoor snacks with his dad when he was a child.

"Oh, Dr. Sami. Apricot juice. You know it will make you poo."

Dr. Sami laughed very loudly and very long.

"Yes indeed. Ha... Ha... Ha... So. Tell me, Munira, how are things at work?"

"I am not happy. You know I had problems with my ovaries. And I now seem to have sensitive bowels because of funny poo."

Dr. Sami shuffled in his seat and looked as intelligent as one could when such bodily matters are mentioned in polite society.

"I am sorry to hear it... Oh, look. Alia's husband seems to have gone..."

"Yes, Dr. Sami. He too has some problems with his intestines and needs to go a lot."

"Oh... I am sorry to hear it... I say Alia... Happy birthday old bean. How are you enjoying it?"

"I am all right now, aren't I Munira? I had a bad day. Kept needing the toilet all the time. I don't know what was wrong."

Dr. Sami was engulfed with a strong sense of despair as he turned to Elaine and suggested that they might want to visit the lovely balcony overlooking the even lovelier scenery.

Suddenly, all those around the table dived on to the large plate of dates. Dr. Sami felt a huge sense of relief as he too took a handful and started eating voraciously whilst listening to the call to prayer.

"Oh Dr. Sami! Look Munira, he really loves his dates. You love your dates. Hey? Be careful because you will need to go a lot tomorrow. Especially with the apricot juice on top."

Dr. Sami laughed uproariously and turned to Munira and asked her about her life in South Africa.

"I don't miss it. I really don't. I miss my mum and my dad and my sisters and my brothers. But I don't miss the country. Don't like some of the awful things they do. You know, like circumcising girls. Cutting off their clitoris so that they don't enjoy sex later in life. I can not understand that. Can you?"

Dr. Sami turned around and stared into her eyes. They were enormous in a very dark almost leathery face tightly surrounded by a scarf that gave the impression that she had come to the dinner disguised as a very thin dark sausage.

"I mean, Dr. Sami, is it fair to deprive a woman of her right to an orgasm? You tell me that Dr. Sami. An orgasm is an inherent need and right, isn't it?"

Dr. Sami looked up and looked down. He looked right and then looked left. He filled his mouth with a large number of dates and made a face indicative of inability to respond and pointed to his bulging mouth. He turned to Elaine.

"The balcony is lovely. Isn't it Elaine?" He mumbled through a mouthful of dates.

"God Sami. I could kill for a bloody smoke..." she whispered.

"Let's go out and you can have a quick smoke. The fast is now broken."

As they stepped out on to the balcony, Dr. Sami whispered with considerable urgency, "One more word about bodily functions or genitalia and I shall scream."

Elaine laughed blowing smoke in his face as he took a deep breath in preparation for a sigh of incomprehension.

He excused himself and went back to the table.

The meal was largely a quiet affair except for Alia and her husband discussing which contents on their joint plate would cause least congestion in the husband's intestines. Dr. Sami found himself thinking of the beautiful breakfast woman and realised that he too was beginning to enter the bodily function twilight zone and quickly squashed the idea.

He overheard Munira whisper loudly to Alia that she felt so horny tonight. Alia laughed and said something about her husband falling asleep most nights when the need arose.

Fruit was munched cheerfully with full commentary from Munira on its spectacular effect on regularising bowel movements.

Another coffee on the balcony with a cigarette for Elaine ended the tortuous evening. Alia complained of having a gut ache and was helped to her car by her husband who incessantly stroked her cheek with his free hand. Dr. Sami fancied that he heard her breaking wind discreetly as she bent to get into the car and it reminded him of *La Grande Bouffe*.

Everyone piled into their different cars. Munira and her husband drove Dr. Sami and Elaine back to their hotel.

The Dabawis and the Shargawis   Faysal Mikdadi

As Dr. Sami stepped out of the car he was sure that he had heard Munira wishing him a good night after a salutary poo. He dismissed the thought as a figment of his overfed imagination.

After another coffee for him and wine and a cigarette for Elaine, Dr. Sami went to his room and showered.

He quickly got ready for bed in anticipation of his nightly phone call from his wife. He absolutely adored her and meeting her was the only event in his life that made him feel that things were really worthwhile. They had a nightly chat that was basically a repetition of as many ways as possible of saying 'I love you' to each other. This was followed by a chat about what they would do to each other when they met next.

Dr. Sami felt a need to go the toilet and panicked that he would not be able to get to the telephone if it rang. It would be most upsetting to miss the ten o'clock call and break the lovely routine. The dilemma was agonising.

Suddenly he remembered the phone by the bath and ran in with a feeling of genuine ecstasy.

The relief was indescribable. It made him think of Joyce's *Ulysses* and he missed having the newspaper.

The phone rang.

He answered it.

"Hello darling. What are you doing sweetheart?" she asked in that magical voice.

"Doing a poo on the toilet."

"What a coincidence. I am doing the same. I did not want to miss calling you at ten. I know how you like to keep to your little timetable. But thank God for wireless phones... I have been having a bit of a problem all day. Lots of poos... Don't know why..."

The Dabawis and the Shargawis　　　　　**Faysal Mikdadi**

Sense and Sensitivity

Saif sat back in the car. He wiped his brown brow with an already wet handkerchief. Beside him sat Mrs. Smythe-Norton whose white brow shone with the effects of the heat.

As the car slid forward, he mumbled something about being too hot. Mrs. Smythe-Norton nodded agreement and adjusted her large dark glasses.

Occasionally, Saif stole a look at her face. She sat upright with her face staring ahead. The driver asked if the AC was enough.

"No my dear fellow. It's a little warm today. Do turn it up please". Saif spoke confidently and in Arabic. He quickly turned to Mrs. Smythe-Norton and added in English, "Is that all right with you".

"Yes!" she snapped back and sat as stiffly as before.

"I'm looking forward to our visit. It should be interesting." He mused.

" 'Could have been interesting' would cover it better I think," Mrs. Smythe-Norton replied savagely. "It may prove a waste of time given that we are going to be late because you let the car driver go. This is meant to be a goodwill visit."

Saif laughed nervously. "Oh. People are easy going in this part of the world you know. They don't live by the clock."

"Well I do" she bristled. "I have lived in this part of the world for twenty years. People in the Persian Gulf have to understand…"

"Arabian Gulf," said Saif.

"Yeah. Whatever… Lack of punctuality is a form of theft of time. They are stealing somebody else's time."

During the silence that followed, Saif wondered what would make her relax a little. There must be a sensitivity button somewhere that he could press.

"Have you settled down in your new place then?" He asked gently.

"In a manner of speaking. I don't call it home. I am never there. I sleep there. I go to work." Her reply was a series of staccato shots aimed straight at the back of the driver's head.

"And your husband? How is his work going?"

"He is a businessman. He does business all over the place. He is in Jordan today. We are used to travelling widely." That last sentence was accompanied by Mrs. Smythe-Norton holding both her arms out with her hands down and fingers bent in the shape of claws. As she continued her hands stayed aloft with the occasional wavy movement accompanying her rhythmic pronouncements. "He does not sell, you know. He is a consultant. He advises major clients..."

Saif stopped listening. His eyes glazed slightly as his mouth took on a permanent smile of assumed interest.

The silence that followed exhausted both speakers. Especially Saif.

"And your daughter? She was born in these parts, wasn't she and is now a teacher? Hmmm?"

She smiled broadly and looked around. She took her glasses off. Saif fancied that he saw a softening in the eyes. Her claws relaxed and she sat back happily.

"She was in Cambridge you know. She did very well. She did her PGCE. Became a teacher last year. Loves it. Loves it. Absolutely divine. She is good at it. Since a child she wanted to become a teacher. She met me at the airport. In Birmingham. Yes. I came through the customs. The flight was full of Indians. I was the only white woman there. The airport was full of *their* lot. And my daughter said that she thought that we were in Raipur or something like that. Yes. She lives in Henley and, of course, there it is all pukah and all that. Of course, I am only joking."

"Yes, of course India is doing very well economically, isn't it?" Saif said irrelevantly.

"And she was born in Bahrain. But she can't have the Bahraini passport. And that makes her furious. I told her to go to Bahrain and agitate."

Saif tried to look sympathetic with little success and said, "Yes, I see. But you know the British have had the same law since the Immigration Act in the early eighties. It was aimed at the relatives of the Ugandan Asians."

"That's different," she snapped. "And if she married a foreigner her children can't be British because she wasn't born in Britain. Would you believe it?"

Saif replied, "A lot of the Polish immigrants are leaving Britain. Interesting development. I wonder if Indians might leave Dubai. Hmmm?"

"And who is going to do all those jobs that we don't want to do?"

"I see...You lived abroad a lot. Didn't you?"

"India. I was born in India. But I am more British than the British..."

And the car slid into its parking space slowly. Saif turned around to open his door when she held his arm and stayed him gently.

"Thank you for that. I enjoyed it." She whispered.

Saif jumped out of the car. He ran to other side and held the door open for her. She slapped her dark glasses back on and stepped out of the car. Nodding at him holding the door, she walked into the school.

He stood holding the door wandering if he was supposed to wait in the car with the Indian driver.

The Lady by the Pool

Dubai. The most wonderful city in the world. It gives you every conceivable experience possible. It loves you with its sunny days, its constant lively activity and its infinite variety. It hates you with its maddening traffic, dream provoking humidity and its wonderous arrogance of 'nothing is impossible to achieve here' attitude.

Dubai. It has so many faces that you are hard pushed to get to know them all. But somehow, you do. Hospitable. Varied. Funny. Organised. Fast. Modest. Simple. Loveable. Beautiful. Rich. Aloof. Insular. Self engrossed. Disorganised. Slow. Hyperbolic. Complex. Hateful. Ugly. Poor.

Dubai. The most unforgettably varied experience during our short journey on this little earth. Not to have experienced Dubai is as catastrophic as never having loved or been loved. To paraphrase that prominent Lotus Eater, "It's better to have passed through Dubai even just once and seen very little of it than never to have been there at all".

****

"This is disgusting! Disgusting! Do you hear what I say? Absolutely disgusting!"

The Dabawis and the Shargawis   **Faysal Mikdadi**

The speaker was a redoubtable American woman. Tall and powerful, she appeared to dwarf the somewhat rotund little man standing before her in his light coloured suit, white shirt, white tie and a quizzical facial expression on a large brown head.

"What distresses you madam? Can I be of any help?" He asked quietly.

The two stood by the pool in the middle of an almost perfect square. The four sides of the square were four high and looming eight storey buildings. The only exit out of the enclosed square was through one of the four buildings reminiscent of 1960s East Berlin tenement flats. Although there was enough day light left, the square felt dark because the four claustrophobic buildings gave the impression of a spacious and drab prison yard from whence there was no possibility of an escape. Stalag 66.

"This! This!" Shrieked the angry American whose name was Pat Linkinlater. "Surely, Dr. Ahmed, surely you can see how aesthetically ugly these buildings are. How dare the Dubai authorities put us up in a dump like this?"

Dr. Ahmad sorely wanted to explain that his name was Ahmad and not Ahmed. That the Dubai authorities were the client and paid their visiting workers' fees so could do whatever they damn well wanted. That he was not really bothered since school inspections took so much out of one that all one wanted to do was fall into a clean bed for the few hours' sleep allowable before awakening at 5.30 a.m. to prepare for another day of relentless toil.

Instead, Dr. Ahmad smiled and changed the subject.

"Quite. Quite... I have found this delightful Lebanese restaurant a few minutes' walk from here. They serve a wonderful Falafel sandwich there, Mrs. Linkinlater..."

"Ms! Ms! Please. Ms! If you don't mind. My husband does not own me, contrary to what some may think in this God foresaken outpost."

Dr. Ahmad smiled, whimpered a little and made a great show of welcoming a newly arrived British inspector.

"Ah! Mr. Palmer. So lovely to see you again. We met in Salisbury last time. St. Joseph's I believe... I was just telling Ms. Linkinlater that I have discovered this delightful place called 'The Lebanese Village'. Serves a wonderful Falafel sandwich..."

The Dabawis and the Shargawis   **Faysal Mikdadi**

"Hello Ahmed... Didn't expect to see *you* in this neck of the woods. Lebanese you said? Can't stand the crap they serve. And no bloody alcohol I suppose?"

"No, Mr. Palmer. I fear not. Mr. Mohammad, the proprietor, does not allow alcohol on his premises."

"Bloody musies!" said Mr. Palmer grimacing.

"Disgraceful!!" shouted Ms. Linkinlater walking away with a circular gesture of her arm taking in the four high buildings. She entered the building leading out to the road. Mr. Palmer sauntered indifferently towards the dining area.

Dr. Ahmad stood by the pool wondering what to do next with his brief few minutes of freedom before dinner as dusk descended into darkness.

He sat down and looked up at the little bit of sky that could be just discerned in the opening at the top of the high square created by the four buildings.

****

The rather stark dining room stood on the first floor of one side of the square. To get to it the visitor needed to walk out into the square, itself built one floor

The Dabawis and the Shargawis   **Faysal Mikdadi**

above the ground floor where stood the hotel car park and large drab reception.

About a dozen school inspectors were in the dining room. They sat in groups of between two and four at a table in an arrangement of four tables forming an almost regimented perfect square.

Dr. Ahmad entered the room and took a few seconds to allow his eyes to adjust after the pitch darkness that he had just walked through. His legs ached from bumping into a couple of tables by the swimming pool.

English was spoken by all the inspectors who were mainly either American or British with two Indian women.

At one table sat three white men in grey suits heatedly discussing Cricket. They were deep in some debate about "winner takes all..." and something do do with "one million dollars".

At the second table sat four white women quietly chatting about inspections.

At the third table sat a very quiet pair who occasionally whispered to each other.

The fourth table had three women. One in a Sari, a second who had very blonde hair and who distinctly displayed Indian facial features and a third who was, judging by her accent, clearly American.

Dr. Ahmad walked over to the three cricketers.

"Good evening Mr. Matthews."

"Evening Ahmed."

Dr. Ahmad looked at the other two and smiled.

"Good evening," he said.

"Hummph…" grunted one.

"D'do?" spat the other.

"We have worked together before. Hillsborough. An academy. You're one of Her Majesty's Inspectors…" smiled Dr. Ahmad.

"Ye-e-e-s. I seem to remember you looking at some Arabian or whatever it was..."

Dr. Ahmad smiled and wondered what the 'I' In HMI might really stand for. He eyed the empty chair and thought better of it as the three men turned away and resumed their heated discussion on cricket.

****

The four women looked at Dr. Ahmad and one of them smiled broadly.

"You're Dr. Ahmad, aren't you?"

"Yes madam..."

"Oh, please call me Jill. I've heard so much about you. From Carole. You remember her?"

"Of course," shouted Dr. Ahmad excited at hearing the name of someone he liked amidst such a cold and hostile group. "Wonderful lady. Wonderful. I had the estimable privilege of working with her very recently... Wonderful..."

Jill looked around at her three colleagues who smiled and nodded vigorously at Dr. Ahmad, reminding him of those plastic birds hooked on the rim of a glass and constantly pecking at its contents.

****

Dr. Ahmad looked toward the quiet pair and noticed that the man had a French novel beside him. He craned to read its title – he could clearly see Hugo's *Les Misérables*. He looked at his partner and thought that she had a gentle smile until her eye caught his and she gave a momentary grimace. He recognised her from an inspection that he had led in Birmingham. She was a lay inpector called Margaret. He liked her, if he remembered rightly. She was petite with long silky hair and gentle little features. She had large kind eyes. Dr. Ahmad turned to the fourth table with the two Indian and one American women.

"Dr. Ahmad, do join us. Do please..." sang out the American.

"Most kind of you Mrs. Skyrme," chuckled the relieved doctor.

"Oh, Dr. Ahmad. Call me Julie..."

"Thank you," and he wanted to add, "call me Dr. Ahmad if you please."

"As I was saying," continued Julie Skyrme as Dr. Ahmad ponderously placed his round body in the chair to her left. "As I was saying, the hotel is awful. Would you believe it, they serve instant coffee. I ask you. And, I feel threatened. This is a red light district. It is in the guide books. There are prostitutes out there. I am too frightened to go out after dark."

Dr. Ahmad wanted to tell the three women about his evening walk coming back from the small supermarket with his individual little cups of filtered coffee. He had been stopped by a very attractive small woman with long silky black hair and the biggest and deepest eyes that he had ever seen.

"Good evening, madam," he had pleasantly intoned.

"Hello. I come to your hotel room. I give you good time. Five hundred only".

"No, madam," he had replied jocularly. "Five hundred is too little. I charge at least two thousand for the basic service, you know."

The prostitute had stepped back. For a few seconds, she had looked a little annoyed. Suddenly, she had laughed out loudly and had put her arm through his.

"Come on, sir. You funny. I like. I do for nothing."

Dr. Ahmad had slowly disengaged himself, taken her hand, shaken it gently saying, "No, thank you, madam. You have a lovely evening."

As he had walked off briskly he had fancied that he could still hear her chuckling.

"Yes. Prostitutes." Julie Skyrme was intoning rather loudly. "What do you think, Dr. Ahmad."

"What madam? What do I think of prostitutes? They are very pretty on the whole..."

The two Indian women laughed. Julie joined in before launching again.

"The food is ghastly. Awful. And we have discovered that the pay is different. Some of us get a lot more than others, and some get a lot less..." she added glancing at the two Indian women.

The Dabawis and the Shargawis   **Faysal Mikdadi**

Dr. Ahmad looked appropriately surprised. Deciding from the expression on Julie's face that surprise was not the appropriate response, he quickly changed his expression to extreme shock. Feeling this to be too much the other way, he moderated it with speedy nods which instantly gave him the look of one of those nodding dogs sitting on the back shelves of some British cars.

"This morning," whispered the first Indian woman," the car was half an hour too early…"

Dr. Ahmad caught Margaret's eye and smiled at her. She nodded almost imperceptively without smiling. He wondered if she remembered him from Birmingham. They had had a good laugh with him showing her how to write her name in Arabic.

One of the cricketers shouted out, "You're lucky. Our bugger was half an hour late. We missed assembly and part of the first lesson. Bloody Indian drivers…"

Dr. Ahmad smiled at the two Indian women ingratiatingly.

Another cricketer looked up through red eyes and leered, rather than smiled, at everybody. "I don't know why the Dubai authorities want their schools inspected. If we were in Britain, we would put the whole lot into Special Measures. Damn abominable provision all round."

One of the four women nodded vigourously and added. "You're right of course John. You see, Arabs can't get organised. Teachers talk too much, don't plan, don't differentiate and students are compliant. Not an idea of what independent learning is or what assessment for learning is..."

"All they can do is memorise the bloody Qur'an. They don't even know what it means." The speaker was another of the four women. "Today, several fell asleep during lessons, would you believe it?" She looked around for confirmation and her eyes landed on Julie who instantly held forth.

"Claustrophobic buildings, awful rooms, ugly décor, bad food, disorganisation and prostitutes everywhere..." began Julie Skyrme. "I haven't seen anything like it since Nicaragua. I'll tell you what... I am not coming back."

"Nor I!" shouted a cricketer.

"Nor I!" shouted another. "Bloody Arabs..."

****

"It's not as bad as all that..." said a quiet, almost inaudible voice. It came from the man with the French novel.

"What?" screeched Julie Skyrme.

"What did you say?" menaced a cricketer.

"It's not all that bad," said French novel a little more boldly.

There was a brief interminable silence such as one imagines precedes a cataclysmic nuclear explosion.

Dr. Ahmad looked again at Margaret and smiled. She smiled back. He fancied that he caught a glimpse of recognition in her large eyes. She obviously just remembered Birmingham and their happy Arabic lesson. He felt a gentle wave of excitement rising within him.

French novel surveyed the occupants of the four tables and spoke quietly but confidently. "The rooms are clean. It's quiet. You have all you need. The food is all right. The pay is good..."

Another silence ensued but was immediately followed by a cataclysmic explosion coming in from all directions.

Dr. Ahmad looked at the waiter, exaggeratedly mouthed the word 'coffee', mimed the action of drinking from a cup with one hand whilst holding the saucer in the other, and pointed toward the swimming pool square. The waiter smiled and nodded.

Dr. Ahmad got up amidst the chorus wondering if, had angry words been black smoke, he would ever find the door out to the square with the swimming pool. He gently ambled his way out of the dining area and into the prison square as the clamour grew louder and louder.

****

Dr. Ahmad sat in the semi darkness by the pool, breathed in deeply and let out a prolonged sigh of relief. He wished that Carole were there to put this particular house in order and join in his laughter at the complainants. He could hardly see anything but shifting soft shadows made more ghostly by the reflections from the water dancing on the walls.

He thought of his immortal beloved back in England. She would be sitting in their warm front room, surrounded by their beloved books and watching the high Eucalyptus tree as it gently swayed in the autumn breeze whilst the garden silently sank into the darkening dusk. He suddenly missed her terribly, missed his little study and the few whooshing and susurating trees whose secret langauge only he understood.

"Hello," said someone who was immediately recognisable as Margaret despite the darkness. One could not mistake the petite body, long silky hair and soft voice.

The doctor put his half drunk cup of coffee down and jumped up.

"Good evening. How lovely of you to come over. Do join me."

Margaret sat down with only the weak poolside light behind her making it even more difficult for the doctor to see her changing facial expressions properly. This only increased his mounting excitement. Despite the gloom, he fancied that he could see her big eyes and distant smile.

"Quite a lot of noise in there. It is difficult not to get sucked into all this unhappiness. Don't like the rooms. Don't like the food. Don't like the pay. Don't like the work..." He trailed off smiling into the semi darkness trying desperately to fathom her expression.

"Not happy?" asked Margaret.

"Well, no, old girl. They were really going at it hammer and tongs...".

"Not happy?" she repeated.

"No," and Dr. Ahmad suddenly felt drained and wanted to change the subject. "Do you remember when we met last?"

"Yes."

"I enjoyed it. It was really nice." He added politely thinking of how cheerful Margaret had been during such a difficult inspection and how they had laughed at her clumsy attempts to write her name in Arabic. His hand had almost touched hers and the world had felt good then.

"Me too..."

A long silence followed.

Suddenly Margaret took the doctor's hand and squeezed it hard. He pulled back.

"I say, steady on old girl..."

"Come," she said taking his hand again. "I come your room. Give you good time. No money. You make me laugh and I like you..."

Dr. Ahmad jumped up realising the embarrassing misunderstanding. A man stepped out of the shadows and walked towards their table.

"Excuse me sir. Is this lady disturbing you?"

"What?" shouted the doctor as he fell exhausted into his chair.

"Is this lady disturbing you? Is this lady with you? If this lady is going to your room, then I will need to see her passport, sir..."

Dr. Ahmad saw the woman stiffen and could almost smell her fear despite the darkness. He looked from her to the man and from the man to her but could only see two dark shapes. He took a deep breath.

"This lady, sir," he said slowly and imperiously. "This lady, sir, is my most esteemed guest. She is here at my invitation to have a quiet cup of coffee with me by the pool. Would you please make sure that we get two coffees my friend?"

"Yes, of course, sir," replied the security guard and backed off.

Coffee was served and quietly sipped. Nothing was said in the awful darkness. Noise of a heated argument could still be heard coming from the dining room. Dr. Ahmad wished that he were back in there in the safety of the ugly familiarity.

"Thank you sir. Thank you. I frightened. I go now. I leave you alone now. I go now..."

Dr. Ahmad stood up.

"No madam. I will walk out with you. This way please..."

He held her by the elbow and steered her into the hotel. They walked into the light of the large reception area. He led her gently towards the exit looking straight ahead and turning neither right nor left. He walked slowly and with as much dignity as his splay feet could muster.

The security guard was standing by the exit door with the three receptionists.

The doctor gently ushered the woman out. On the pavement, he could feel, rather than see, the eight eyes burning into his back.

He took the woman by the elbow even more firmly and steered her away from the hotel.

"This is for you. It's very little. But it's all I can afford..."

"No. I no take. You good man. Funny. I no take..."

"Please take it. For me..." he said pressing the dirty crumpled note into her little hand and closing it over it.

"I really wish you the best, love..." he whispered as he thought of his home, books and trees.

He walked briskly back to the hotel, ran up the few steps and burst into the foyer.

"Evening. Evening." He sang to the three Indian receptionists and the security guard who stood there smiling broadly at him and nodding their heads cheerfully. He waved at Mrs. Linkinlater who was absorbed reading the *Gulf News* and chuckling to herself. He shrugged his shoulders and walked on briskly.

As he stood by the lift, he fancied that he heard the continuing clamour from the dining area. And he was again happy to be out of it.

"Awful hotel," he mused. "Awful... I'm so lucky...So lucky!"

The Dabawis and the Shargawis   **Faysal Mikdadi**

Dubai Days©

A Musical

The Dabawis and the Shargawis   **Faysal Mikdadi**

List of contents

The Dabawis and the Shargawis   **Faysal Mikdadi**

Music: The tune of Land of Hope and Glory from Elgar's

Pomp and Circumstance March No. 1 in D major Opus 39

Music: Habeebi Habeebti

Interlude 3

Lyrics: Habeebi Habeebti

Curtain

Characters

In Order of Appearance

Richard: An old man probably in his mid seventies or maybe a little younger.

Samir: Richard's youngest son probably in his mid twenties or early thirties.

Lina: A beautiful young woman of 1960s Dubai. Darwish's and Samira's daughter. Richard's wife. Samir's mother.

Samira: Lina's mother and Samir's grandmother. She is also Darwish's wife and Richard's mother in law.

Darwish: Lina's father. Samira's husband. Richard's father in law. Samir's grandfather.

Richard: As a young man.

Suggested Stage Set

Entry / Exit Right

Plant

Hanging on the wall
are fisherman's net,
pearling baskets, the
odd long oar and a
few other implements
of workers by the sea
specialising in fishing
and pearl diving

Plant

Plant

Plant

Screen hanging over
house wall at the back
of the stage on which
are projected images of
old and modern Dubai

Entry / Exit Left

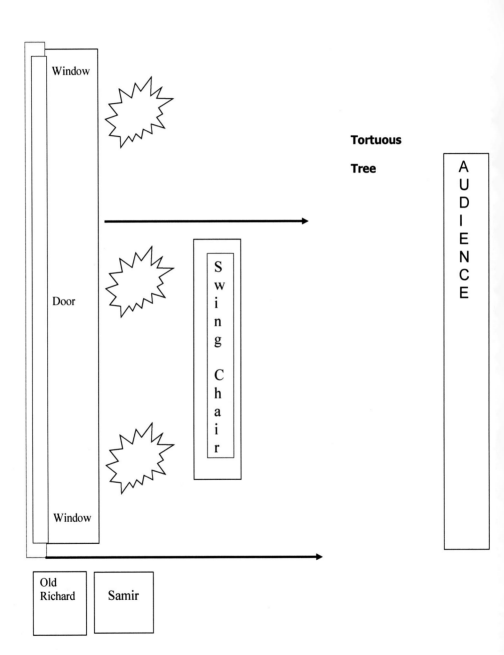

Swing Seat / Chair Suggestion

The Dabawis and the Shargawis   **Faysal Mikdadi**

Scene 1

[Two old wooden high backed chairs stand stage left. The spotlight is on

them. The light slowly grows to encompass an empty stage. Suspended

above towards the back of the stage is a wide screen with a desert view.

Ideally, the scenery moves slowly until Richard walks in from the right. He

walks very slowly across the stage and sits on one of the two chairs.

Richard is an old man. As he sits down, the desert scene freezes part

behind him and part to his left across the stage. All through this opening

scene there is music. The 'Overture' music starts with gentle almost

distant strumming on the Oud (seven-chorded Arab lute). This is first

joined, then replaced by, the evocative tones of the al-Na'y (Arab pipe).

The music should be solemn but not sad, a kind of reflective background

whilst evoking the Arab world and its landscape. Once Richard has sat

down for a while, the music slowly fades away. The desert vista stays all

through this scene. Bubbly happy excited Arabic music strikes up as a

handsome young man walks in. Nothing necessarily indicates directly that

he is Richard's youngest son. He is round about 25 or 30 years old, fresh

looking and full of life. His name is Samir. He walks, half prancing to the

music, towards his old father. He reaches his father's chair and dances

around him a few times. Richard looks up and smiles broadly. He struggles

up and Samir helps him. The two men perform a brief Lebanese dance - It is called Debka - in slowish steps. Samir solicitously and very gently holds

his father who dances clumsily and with obvious physical discomfort. The

music stops. The two men look at each other, laugh loudly and hug as

they greet each other joyfully. They both sit down on their respective

chairs].

Samir: Marhaba ya baba.

Richard: Welcome son. Welcome.

Samir: Kifak baba?

Richard: Alhamdulillah my boy. It is all in His hands.

Samir: Shoo ya baba? Hey dad. I've been thinking.

Richard: A dangerous habit my boy. [He laughs. Samir looks a little

confused, then, as the penny drops, he too laughs].

Samir: So you came here from England in the early sixties. That's where

we got to yesterday. So, did you miss England, dad?

Richard: [Pensive for a while]. I don't know my boy. I missed my mum I

suppose. Not England. [Reminisces awhile]. England had lost its way. It

was morally bankrupt. Like today. So no change there then. [He laughs

gently].

Samir: Today England is financially bankrupt. [They both laugh uneasily].

But, dad, there was nothing to come to here. These fast developments

had not even started yet. The place was arid, hostile and virtually barren.

Richard: May be. May be, my son. But, things were beginning a little bit. Nothing much yet, but still enough to keep us busy.

Samir: Tell me about it, dad.

Richard: It is a story of trials and tribulations my boy. Of ecstasy and heartache. Of meetings and partings. Do you really want to hear it? Your generation knows no disappointment. It is surging ahead with all due speed. You are full of optimism.

Samir: But dad, your early life, trials and tribulations are what made me what I am. The more I know of your life, the more sense would mine make.

Richard: All right son. Let me tell you a story. Listen to me. Pay attention. Look at me and see with me the story I shall tell you.

[Richard raises his arm and points towards the screen desert scene and draws an arc across the stage. As he does so, the desert scene moves and old Dubai slowly appears with its few clumsily built houses and pitched Arab tents by the beach. On the stage begin to appear characters in his story].

Richard: Ah my boy. Memories come flooding in. [Sings gently].

The Dabawis and the Shargawis   **Faysal Mikdadi**

Memories

Life's a long dream

With so little as would seem

But, at my age,

I know that it's a page

Only I can read,

Back to the very first seed.

My memories are what made me

The man that you can see.

My childhood, boyhood and years

Of growing love and subsiding fears.

Look with me at these pictures

There, there, can you see?

Like you son, I was once young

With no thought of ever growing old.

Full of life.

Full of strength.

Full of care free ambition.

And waiting, waiting, waiting.

The Dabawis and the Shargawis   **Faysal Mikdadi**

Waiting for love

Which, like time, creeps up on you,

Overtakes you,

And gives you no choice.

I fell in love

And now I'm old.

The bonus of life was my love,

The meaning of living was my love.

The insignificance of age was my love.

For it's the only thing conquering all, my love.

And holding it all together, my love.

Making it all sweet and happy, my love.

[As Richard gently sings 'Memories', the scene changes as the image of

old Dubai freezes. The stage is lit up and shows a small courtyard of a

pretty rustic home].

Scene 2

[The courtyard of an old Dubai rustic home. A beautiful young woman walks in as Richard's song nears it end. All Arab women in this play always appear wearing a 'shela' (local Dubai headscarf) and local dress. Austere without being forbidding. The 'shela' is worn loosely. Women keep adjusting it in a slightly provocative or potentially flirtatious gesture. All through the rest of the play, it may be advisable to let Richard and Samir remain seated quietly miming a speaker and a listener. Lina, the beautiful young woman, walks around the yard looking almost as if she could hear the song. She touches various bits hanging on the walls: a fisherman's net, pearling baskets, the odd long oar and a few other implements of workers by the sea specialising in fishing and pearl diving. The set also includes a swing seat made entirely of wood ornately carved. This will be used during young Richard and Lina's duet in Scene 3 and all through the play. As the music comes to an end, Richard's song is over and he turns to face Samir full on. Gentle music background continues after Richard stops singing. The music is evocative of the past, of remembering, of nostalgia].

Lina: Mama! Mama!

[A slightly corpulent but still pretty woman emerges from the little house. She is dressed in colourful national dress with the usual headscarf constantly being adjusted on her head].

Samira: Habeebti! Habeebti! What is it my little bird?

[Lina stands still and stares at her mother in apparent terror. Her mother looks at her. For a while, the two are frozen on either side of the stage. Gentle insistent music warns the audience of impending emotional turmoil. Samira puts her arms out and Lina runs into them like a little child].

Lina: Oh mama! Mama!

Samira: Hey! Hey! Shoo fee ya habeebti? What is the matter with my little bird? I have not heard you sing for days. Tell your mother my little Bulbul. Nothing can be that bad. Do I not remember the pain you caused me at your birth?

[Samira laughs happily and holds Lina at arms length. Lina laughs].

Samira: That's better. And don't I remember the pain you caused at your conception?

Lina: [In shock] Mama! [She hugs her mother and hides her pretty face in her neck].

Samira: Ah! My little delicate flower. It is shy. You are a grown woman now. Soon you will have a husband to make you uncomfortable.

Lina: Mama! Is it awful?

Samira: That's what we tell them to keep them on their toes. To make 'em feel guilty. It doesn't work mind, they still behave like apes. In reality, my little lamb, it is so special.

Lina: Oh, mama! Mama! I love him so!

[Samira jumps back in horror letting go of Lina who stares at her fearfully. She stares at her daughter for a long time before she dramatically holds the following exchange with her].

Samira: Love? Love? Him? Him?

Lina: Yes mama. Love. Him.

Samira: Him?

Lina: Him.

Samira: that Bedu.

Lina: Mama?

Samira: Granted he has a great manly appearance. His eyes, once made up, look striking. Oh, my daughter, al taraf al aghar, so tempting.

Lina: Who are you talking about, mama?

Samira [Not listening to her daughter]: Yes. He is a handsome specimen. Those eyes are to die for. Indeed, Omar is beautiful.

Lina [Quite clearly shocked]: Omar? Omar? Mama. It is not Omar.

Samira: Oh, what a relief. What a relief. The Bedu are a great people no doubt but they can't sit still long enough. We are city dwellers, my daughter.

Lina: No, mama. It is Richard. Richard I love, mama.

[The silence is electrifying. To Samira, the world has as good as ended. As she steps back looking at the terrified Lina, the distant strains of Elgar's *Pomp and Circumstance March No. 1 in D major Opus 39* can be heard – the tune of *Land of Hope and Glory* only. This tune goes up and down in volume during the explosion that follows].

Samira: Aiee! Aiee! Aiee! Allah! Allah come and take me now. An Englishman. And what is wrong with Omar? Not good enough for you? The Bedu are a great people. They are nomadic no doubt. But, they are healthy and hardy because of that. They walk a lot. Mr. Richard is much too old for you anyhow.

Lina: But mama, he is only thirty six. That is just two years older than Omar.

Samira: Ah! At that time of life – two years make men age very quickly.

Lina: Mama, I love him.

Samira: Love? Love? [She is now shrieking hysterically]. Love? And what is there to love? An Englishman? Pale as gone off Saffron. Turns the colour of lobster by mid morning. Soft and flabby. Not an ounce of manhood in him. He walks like a woman. He doesn't eat meat! A vegetarian if you please! More like a vegetable if you ask me. A cauliflower. All wind and no substance.

Lina: Mama, I love him.

Samira: And poor handsome love sick Omar?

Lina: But mama, I love Richard.

Samira: Will you stop repeating that? He does not even speak Arabic.

Lina: Mama, I speak a little English and I'm teaching him Arabic.

Samira: Ah! It's all your father's fault! I told him not to send you to that silly school. I told him that women must not learn to read. They go astray. Ah! Ah! And look what has happened now!

Lina: But mama, I love him.

Samira [Shrieking]: Enough! Enough!

[Lina bursts into heartrending sobs and buries her face in her hands as she collapses on to the swing seat].

Samira: Oh! My little butterfly. Don't cry... [Samira rushes forward with her arms extended and suddenly stops and drops her arms in despair]. No! Do cry! Cry! For you shall not have this infidel. No!!

[Samira sits down on the swing seat and holds Lina against her and strokes her head].

[A handsome and proud looking man, slightly older than Samira, walks in. He is tall and sports a dignified beard. He has a leonine shock of hair which gives him the look of a rather handsome but terrifying predator. He paces up and down as the two women remain seated looking up at him with wide and somewhat apprehensive eyes].

Darwish: What is the matter?

Samira: Nothing ya Abu Lina.

Darwish: Nothing? And for nothing you shriek? And for nothing Bright Eyes is crying? And for nothing she hides her face in her mother's bosom?

Samira: Ya Abu Lina! Ya habeebi. She is upset.

Darwish: Upset?

Samira: Upset.

Darwish: Upset by?

Samira: Upset by affairs of the heart.

Darwish: Stuff and nonsense! Been reading her silly romances again, has she?

Samira: No, husband. She is in love.

Darwish: Love? With Omar? Decent enough chap. Could do worse. Omar is good.

Samira: No husband. With Mr. Richard.

Darwish: Mr. Richard? The English pale face? The shy one? The vegetable eater? The carrot cruncher?

Samira: The same, Abu Lina.

[Samira gets up and manoeuvres her way behind Darwish where she remains for the rest of this scene. Lina stares at her father with wide terrified eyes. Her mother stands slightly behind the father quietly miming to her daughter to keep quiet and not anger her father].

Darwish [In a quiet threatening voice]: Listen daughter. I have been a liberal father. You have received a good education. You have had the freedom to choose in some ways. But for now, do this: Get this nonsense out of your head. When you fall in love, I will, or your mother, should she cease being so soppy, will inform you of the auspicious fact. We will then inform you of the name of the man you have fallen in love with. Soon thereafter we will appoint a date for your wedding. [He turns his back on the two women and faces the audiences]. And then we will await to see

how fruitful you are in continuing your husband's august lineage. [His

back still to the women]. Now go to your room and remain there until I

call you...

[Lina rushes off sobbing. Lights fade off stage. The audience can see

Richard and Samir only with the old Dubai backdrop].

Interlude 1

Samir: Haram ya baba. Poor girl.

Richard: Yes. Poor woman. But those days were different. Not like today's Dubai with its Manhattan skyline and its liberal ways. Oh, my boy. These were harsh days. Harsh. [Old Richard looks at the audience as he continues with the following statement]. And the poor woman who loved me and whom I loved had to do what her father said.

Samir: So, did she marry Omar, baba?

Richard: Shwayeh, shwayeh, my boy. A bit at a time. Let me tell you the sad story my way.

Samir: Okay dad. I'm listening.

Interval

Scene 3

[The same stage set as when Lina first appeared. The stage is empty with
the evocative music from the beginning of Scene 1 softly playing in the
background. The younger Richard walks on. He looks a little furtive.
Tentative. He walks around obviously looking for someone. He looks
through whatever windows that may be accessible. He gently knocks on
one. A short time later, the door opens and Lina comes running out. They
run into each other's arms and stand still as the music slowly fades. They
stand facing each other during the following exchange until they sing their
duet which they do on the swing seat].

Lina: Habeebi!

Richard: Darling!

Lina: Habeebi!

Richard: Darling!

Lina: Habeebi!

Richard [As he is about to speak she holds her hand to his mouth].

Lina: Shshsh. Don't say it. [Lina speaks passable English with a strong
Arabic accent characterised by rolling the letter R and by occasionally
pronouncing words phonetically]. Don't say it. I teach you.

Richard: Teach me.

Lina: Habeebti.

Richard: Habeebi.

Lina [She laughs joyfully at his use of the masculine noun form]: No,

habeebi. You are habeebi. To you, I'm habeebti. Ha-beeb-ti.

Richard: Ha-beeb-ti. [Lina claps her hands with joy]. Habeebti.

Lina: Habeebi!

Richard: Habeebti!

Lina: Habeebi!

Richard: Habeebti!

[They hug as the music for their duet strikes up. The duet should be sung

with the two sitting on the wooden swing seat. Richard occasionally gets

up and walks around the swing seat touching Lina's hand(s) and / or

shoulders. Lina adjusts and readjusts her shela at various points when

young Richard sings. Her adjustment could be slightly coy and flirtatious.

The two sing separately and join each other in this choreographed love

duet].

Habeebi Habeebti

Lina: Habeebi.

The Dabawis and the Shargawis   **Faysal Mikdadi**

Richard: Habeebti.

Lina: Habeebi, Habeebi.

Richard: Habeebti. Habeebti.

Both at the same time: **Lina**: Habeebi. Habeebi.

                                  Richard: Habeebti. Habeebti.

Richard: When I first saw you,

I knew what love could do.

When I first saw you,

My heart yearned for you.

Lina: Life was so bleak,

And I ever so meek.

Then you came along

And my life's become a song.

Richard: Habeebti, then sing with me.

Sing of this love you see.

Of all you and I feel

And let this kiss be my seal.

[They kiss fleetingly].

Lina: Habeebi. Ah! Habeebi.

Kiss me again, habeebi.

Then let us sing

And fly on love's wing.

[They kiss fleetingly].

Both: We are one because of love.

All our pasts were for this.

No parting will there ever be.

We are one because of love.

Lina: Habeebi.

Richard: Habeebti.

Lina: Habeebi.

The Dabawis and the Shargawis   **Faysal Mikdadi**

Richard: Habeebti.

Both at the same time: **Lina**: Habeebi. Habeebi.

                              Richard: Habeebti. Habeebti.

Richard: When I first saw you,

I knew what love could do.

When I first saw you,

My heart yearned for you.

Lina: Life was so bleak,

And I ever so meek.

Then you came along

And my life's become a song.

Richard: Habeebti, then sing with me.

Sing of this love you see.

Of all you and I feel

And let this kiss be my seal.

[They kiss fleetingly].

Lina: Habeebi. Ah! Habeebi.

Kiss me again, habeebi.

Then let us sing

And fly on love's wing.

[They kiss fleetingly].

Both: We are one because of love.

All our pasts were for this.

No parting will there ever be.

We are one because of love.

Lina: Habeebi.

Richard: Habeebti.

Lina: Habeebi.

Richard: Habeebti.

The Dabawis and the Shargawis   **Faysal Mikdadi**

Both at the same time: **Lina**: Habeebi. Habeebi.

                                 Richard: Habeebti. Habeebti.

[As the music comes to an end they separate and stand staring at each

other].

Richard: Nothing will ever separate us.

Lina: Habeebi. I'm so frightened. My dad is not happy.

Richard [Defiant]: I'm not frightened of anyone. I love you.

[Darwish's voice makes them scurry off stage whimpering in fright as a

stark contrast to Richard's youthful defiance. They exit at two opposing

points].

Darwish: Wife! Wife! Ya Samira! [He walks about the courtyard in search

of his wife. He raises his arms in the air and drops them in despair]. Ya

Allah! What are we to do? Aiiee! Who would have daughters? Ya Allah!

Help us in our hour of need. What are we to do? The girl loves this foreign

boy. But, we have our customs and our traditions. Traditions and customs.

[Darwish shouts the following imperiously]. A'datoona wa taqaleedoona!

A'datoona wa taqaleedoona! He sings.

The Dabawis and the Shargawis   **Faysal Mikdadi**

Our Traditions and Our Customs

Traditions!

Hundreds of years!

Customs!

Hundreds of years!

Time does not change 'em.

Not even her love for him.

Our traditions!

Our customs!

My father before me.

His before him.

And his before him.

From oldest times.

Traditions!

Hundreds of years!

Customs!

Hundreds of years!

The Dabawis and the Shargawis   **Faysal Mikdadi**

Time does not change 'em.

Not even her love for him.

I think today.

And my thoughts are

One thousand years old.

Good enough then,

Good enough now.

From oldest times.

Traditions!

Hundreds of years!

Customs!

Hundreds of years!

Time does not change 'em.

Not even her love for him.

These traditions.

These customs.

From time immemorial

Are what make us

What we are

The Dabawis and the Shargawis   **Faysal Mikdadi**

And always will be.

Traditions!

Hundreds of years!

Customs!

Hundreds of years!

Time does not change 'em.

Not even her love for him.

And now love pays a visit

And they want

To change our ways.

Never! Never! Never!

Our traditions and our customs

Are here to stay.

Traditions!

Hundreds of years!

Customs!

Hundreds of years!

Time does not change 'em.

Not even her love for him.

[Darwish marches off shaking his head. Exit right. His wife, Samira, comes in left].

Samira: A'datoona wa taqaleedoona! Traditions! Traditions! What of love? Your traditions will crush my baby's heart and break her gentle spirit. You and your traditions! But, we married according to our traditions... [She sits on the swing seat]. Oh, I remember it so well. When my father told me I was to marry Darwish, I cried all night. I didn't like his moustache. [She laughs to herself]. I was so innocent. I didn't like his moustache! Well, I was in for a shock... [She laughs again]. A pleasant shock for I grew to love the gentle fool. I grew to love him dearly. But my little baby is so unhappy...

[This next song is sung primarily by Samira. During the song, her statements are responded to by both Darwish off stage right and by old Richard to the left. Darwish pushes for tradition and old Richard pushes for love. The tunes for both men could either be the same as the one supporting Samira's song. Alternatively, Darwish's responses could use the tune of his earlier song 'Our Traditions and Our Customs'. Old Richard's responses could be supported by the tune used in his 'Habeebi Habeebti'].

Love over Traditions

Samira: when I first met him

I feared him so.

Our traditions made fear go.

Darwish [Off stage right]: Traditions!

Hundreds of years!

Customs!

Hundreds of years!

Time does not change 'em.

Not even her love for him.

Old Richard [From his seat stage left]: When I first saw you,

I knew what love could do.

When I first saw you,

My heart yearned for you.

Samira: And in time I grew to love him.

So traditions did stay

And take my fears away.

The Dabawis and the Shargawis   **Faysal Mikdadi**

Darwish [Off stage right]: Traditions!

Hundreds of years!

Customs!

Hundreds of years!

Time does not change 'em.

Not even her love for him.

Old Richard [From his seat stage left]: When I first saw you,

I knew what love could do.

When I first saw you,

My heart yearned for you.

Samira: But then, I never fell in love

I fell into fear

With that gentle dear.

Darwish [Off stage right]: Traditions!

Hundreds of years!

Customs!

Hundreds of years!

Time does not change 'em.

Not even her love for him.

The Dabawis and the Shargawis   **Faysal Mikdadi**

Old Richard [From his seat stage left]: When I first saw you,

I knew what love could do.

When I first saw you,

My heart yearned for you.

Samira: But times have changed

And my little bird loves him so

And can't see to let him go.

Darwish [Off stage right]: Traditions!

Hundreds of years!

Customs!

Hundreds of years!

Time does not change 'em.

Not even her love for him.

Old Richard [From his seat stage left]: When I first saw you,

I knew what love could do.

When I first saw you,

My heart yearned for you.

All three together:

Samira: what can I do now?

Traditions or love, love or traditions.

Surely, my little bird can choose.

Darwish [Off stage right]: Traditions!

Hundreds of years!

Customs!

Hundreds of years!

Time does not change 'em.

Not even her love for him.

Old Richard [From his seat stage left]: When I first saw you,

I knew what love could do.

When I first saw you,

My heart yearned for you.

[Samira sighs deeply and walks off stage left, just as young Richard and Lina come in holding hands].

Richard: Habeebti Lina.

Lina: Habeebi! [She puts both her hands in his and looks at them]. Oh!

Look, I need to paint my nails.

Richard: What?

Lina: I need to paint my nails…

Richard: Where did that come from?

Lina [coquettishly]: I don't know… What? What?

Richard: Lina habeebti. Shoo behebek. How I love you.

Lina: And I you habeebi.

Richard: Do you also need to do your toenails?

Lina [laughing coyly]: Stop it, habeebi.

Richard: You are like a butterfly. Your mind flutters from place to place.

[Lina laughs gently and hugs him. As he sings the next song, she moves away from, and returns to, him according to the words of the song. He occasionally puts his hands out as if he is gently catching a butterfly which he brings to his face to sing his song before he lets the butterfly go in the penultimate stanza].

Flutterby

Flit.

Flit.

The Dabawis and the Shargawis

Faysal Mikdadi

Flit.

Go here.

Go there.

Flit.

Flit.

Flit.

Oh, my little butterfly,

I see you flutter by.

Full of carefree love.

Flit.

Flit.

Flit.

Go here.

Go there.

Flit.

Flit.

Flit.

You became a butterfly,

And I heard you sigh

The Dabawis and the Shargawis   Faysal Mikdadi

So full of love for me.

Flit.

Flit.

Flit.

Go here.

Go there.

Flit.

Flit.

Flit.

Stay! Stay! Beautiful butterfly,

Don't go so high

Stay so full of our love.

Flit.

Flit.

Flit.

Go here.

Go there.

Flit.

Flit.

The Dabawis and the Shargawis   **Faysal Mikdadi**

Flit.

Flit as you will my butterfly

But in one thing

Remain constant:

In our never ending love.

Flit.

Flit.

Flit.

Go here.

Go there.

Flit.

Flit.

Flit.

[The screen hanging in the background could show images of butterflies

flitting on and off a large local Bougainvillaea draped over a wall.

Butterflies could also been seen flitting across the stage].

Interlude 2

Samir: Did it end well, baba?

Richard: My boy, you are impatient. A story has a chronology. It moves forward step by step. You will know by and by, son.

Samir: I know. But it makes me impatient. If this happened to me, dad, I would marry the woman I love, whether her father liked it or not! It's my life...

Richard: Ah, the modern world. You are lucky my boy. Lucky. Let me tell you the rest of this very sad story.

Samir: Yes, baba.

Richard: Ah, my boy, if only I had my time again...

[Old Richard walks on to the stage during this song. He touches various parts such as the swing seat, the fishing tackle hanging up, the tree and so on. He does this nostalgically as if he were gently visiting his past life].

If Only I Had My Time Again

When you lose something – anything,

You search and search,

Then you find it – somewhere.

The Dabawis and the Shargawis

Faysal Mikdadi

But time lost is time gone.

You only get the one go.

After that – there is no turning back.

If only I had my time again.

So that you can never wane.

And love could eternal be.

Oh! Just a second chance – you see.

If only I have my time again.

I would still fall in love

But I should carry you away

And keep traditions at bay.

If only I had my time again.

Life would've not been in vain.

I should love her with all my might

And customs would lose after a brief fight.

If only I had my time again.

I would have been born here

And then chivalrous I would be

The Dabawis and the Shargawis   **Faysal Mikdadi**

In uniting her – one, both her and me.

If only I had my time again

I would have sung of my love

And poured poetry in her ear

To her soft voice intoning, "Yes dear!"

If only I had my time again.

If only I had my time again.

If only I had my time again.

[Old Richard walks back to his seat as the music fades off. He sits facing

Samir as the next scene starts].

Scene 4

[The same stage set as the previous scenes. Lina is sitting on the swing seat looking a little anxious. She keeps looking both sides of her as if anticipating an arrival (left) and fearing another (right). Her father calls (right). She jumps up almost in terror. She looks left and then right but chooses to go into the house through a small door behind her. Her father keeps calling her name (right). His voice gets louder as he approaches].

Darwish: Lina! Lina! Lina! Daughter. Where are you? Really! What has got hold of that girl?

[Young Richard comes in (left) running into the yard towards the swing seat. As he does so, he is accompanied by gentle distant strains of *Land of Hope and Glory* from Elgar's *Pomp and Circumstance March No. 1 in D major Opus 39*. He sees Darwish who has not yet seen him as he has his back to him. Richard turns around and begins to tiptoe towards exit left. He stops. He turns around and takes a very deep breath as the music stops].

Richard: Sir?

Darwish: Huh? What the devil are you doing here, boy?

Richard: I'm sorry to disturb you sir. Please may I speak to you?

Darwish: Arab hospitality is my master here. It demands that I receive you.

[Darwish walks toward the swing seat and throws himself down with an exasperated loud sigh].

Richard: Thank you sir.

Darwish: Don't thank me, sir. Thank our traditions and customs.

[Darwish hums the song '*Our Traditions and Our Customs*' softly as he sits looking around him indifferently. Background score of the song supports Darwish's humming. Richard walks about during his next long speech. He occasionally stops before Darwish and continues to talk before resuming his walking about. During Richard's speech, Darwish, who has stopped humming '*Our Traditions and Our Customs*', fidgets and occasionally snorts loudly].

Richard: Thank you sir. Sir, I love your daughter with all my heart and with every fibre of my being. I wish to ask for your permission to marry her, sir. I will be able to look after her. I am now an engineer and I work for a British oil company, sir. I have good prospects. I would be in a position to care for my wife and for our children, sir. I love Lina and I think that she loves me, sir. Please, sir, give me a chance to make her happy. I would be happy for our children to be brought up in their mother's culture and faith. I would be privileged to learn to speak Arabic, sir. Please, sir, give us a chance for happiness. I will not let you down...

Darwish [Shouts]: Enough! Enough! [He continues in a softer voice as he sees Richard recoiling in fear]. No, my boy. It will not happen. It can't happen. Lina will marry one of her own people. And that's final. Go to your people my boy. Go and live with your own. It wouldn't work...

[Richard hangs his head down and walks slowly towards exit left. Gentle distant music of '*Habeebi Habeebti* plays softly. Ideally, the music should be romantic, nostalgic and gently sad. It should evoke images of loss, disappointment and lovelessness. As Richard exits left, Darwish stands up and looks at the exit. He stares sadly for a while as the music continues. He shakes his head and slowly exits right].

Interlude 3

Samir: Ah, baba! How sad.

Richard: All love stories are sad. But things turn out right. They always do in life.

Samir: So, dad, what was the outcome of all of this?

Richard: What came out of all of this? Let me see.

[Richard stands up and half talks to his son and half to the audience].

Richard: A deep and abiding love came out of this.

[Samir gets up and helps his father slowly walk on to the stage set toward the swing seat].

Richard: A series of wonderful and unforgettable memories. Endless images of happiness.

[They stop walking and half face the audience].

Richard: Years of happiness lived in endless love.

[Richard looks at his son intently and strokes his face].

Richard: You came out of all of this son.

Samir: You married Lina?

Richard: Yes my boy. Except your mother's name was not Lina. I just changed it to make my story less personal – more universal.

Samir: Baba! You and your poetic licence! Mum always said that you were a story teller at heart.

Richard: And a poet my boy. And a poet. Who could live in the Arab world and not be infected by its beautiful poetry? All Arabs are poets my boy. Ah, my boy. Your mother is always in my heart. Even more so ever since that day her father sought me out at work and brought me to his home. He said that he was moved by my appeal and by his daughter's bitter tears and wanted to give his daughter and I a chance for happiness.

[Samir walks away and sits on the swing chair staring gently at his father. Lina enters right and walks towards old Richard. She is still a young woman].

Habeebi Habeebti

Lina: Habeebi.

Richard: Habeebti.

Lina: Habeebi, Habeebi.

Richard: Habeebti. Habeebti.

Both at the same time: **Lina**: Habeebi. Habeebi.

                                Richard: Habeebti. Habeebti.

Richard: When I first saw you,

I knew what love could do.

When I first saw you,

My heart yearned for you.

Lina: Life was so bleak,

And I ever so meek.

Then you came along

And my life's become a song.

Richard: Habeebti, then sing with me.

Sing of this love you see.

Of all you and I feel

And let this kiss be my seal.

[They kiss fleetingly].

Lina: Habeebi. Ah! Habeebi.

Kiss me again, habeebi.

Then let us sing

And fly on love's wing.

[They kiss fleetingly].

Both: We are one because of love.

All our pasts were for this.

No parting will there ever be.

We are one because of love.

Lina: Habeebi.

The Dabawis and the Shargawis

Faysal Mikdadi

Richard: Habeebti.

Lina: Habeebi.

Richard: Habeebti.

Both at the same time: **Lina**: Habeebi. Habeebi.

                                      Richard: Habeebti. Habeebti.

Richard: when I first saw you,

I knew what love could do.

When I first saw you,

My heart yearned for you.

Lina: Life was so bleak,

And I ever so meek.

Then you came along

And my life's become a song.

Richard: Habeebti, then sing with me.

Sing of this love you see.

Of all you and I feel

And let this kiss be my seal.

[They kiss fleetingly].

Lina: Habeebi. Ah! Habeebi.

Kiss me again, habeebi.

Then let us sing

And fly on love's wing.

[They kiss fleetingly].

Both: We are one because of love.

All our pasts were for this.

No parting will there ever be.

We are one because of love.

Lina: Habeebi.

Richard: Habeebti.

Lina: Habeebi.

Richard: Habeebti.

Both at the same time: **Lina**: Habeebi. Habeebi.

                                    Richard: Habeebti. Habeebti.

[As they sing their love duet '*Habeebi Habeebti*', Richard slowly begins to stand up straight and slowly begins to move as a young man again. As the song reaches its finale, he is, to all intents and purposes, a young man except that he still looks his old age. Behind them the screen displays a slide show of their lives through old pictures showing their marriage, the same rustic home, work, baby Samir...etc... The song fades as the two hold hands facing each other and the curtain comes down].

Curtain

Lightning Source UK Ltd.
Milton Keynes UK
UKOW052150250313

208161UK00001B/84/P